I0580446

REQUITED 2
Susan's Story

Baron Alexander

Wilderwick Press

Forest Row, United Kingdom

Copyright © 2023 by **Baron Alexander**

All rights reserved. No part of this publication may be reproduced, distributed or transmitted in any form or by any means, without prior written permission.

Baron Alexander/Wilderwick Press
Unit 4 Ashdown Court, Lewes Road
Forest Row, East Sussex, RH18 5EZ
United Kingdom
www.baronalexanderbooks.com

Publisher's Note: This is a work of fiction. Names, characters, places, and incidents are a product of the author's imagination. Locales and public names are sometimes used for atmospheric purposes. Any resemblance to actual people, living or dead, or to businesses, companies, events, institutions, or locales is completely coincidental.

Dedicated to Susan

CONTENTS

PART ONE—Umhlanga, South Africa (Feb 1998) .. 1

Hampstead, UK (February 1999)............................ 15

Hampstead, London (February 1999) 29

Twenty Years Later… May 2019 Hampstead, London
.... 43

The Shotgun Shell.. 49

Inspiration 55

Four Months Later… Belsize Park, London (May,
2019) 59

Hampstead, London (May 2019) 73

Eight Months Later…Hampstead, London (2020) .. 79

PART TWO—Brothers Twenty-Three Years
Earlier…Winter, 1997, Winnipeg, Canada 81

Sussex, UK (May 2019)... 95

The Derainier Estate, Sussex (May 2019).............. 103

The Derainier Estate, Sussex (May 2019).............. 113

One Month Later… June onwards, 2019 London and
Greater London 117

Eleven Months Later… Carnaby and Belgravia,
London (June, 2020) 127

Marylebone, London (July, 2020)........................... 137

Aftermath 143

Fourteen Months Earlier… Robert Derainier, aka Bob Day (May 2019) 149

Derainier Estate, Sussex (May, 2019) 155

Tipping Point 165

Park Lane, London (May 2019) 171

Copycat 183

London (May 2019) 187

The Derainier Estate, Sussex (May 2019) 197

Derainier Estate, Sussex Two Months Later… July 2019 205

Eight Months Later… 209

PART ONE—Umhlanga, South Africa (Feb 1998)

Susan sighed as Marcel rolled off her and the two lay under the stars. He was her first and she planned for him to be her last. There was nothing more she wanted from life. Well, maybe a baby or three in time. Her hands traced her body, feeling his warmth inside her. She massaged her skin and curled into him, wanting to hold him until the sun rose.

Marcel pulled his arm and her closer to him. Lying on a blanket on the beach in Umhlanga was not a safe option. But their day was too intense to end. The force that held them together was stronger than either of them had experienced before. Their toes touched as they lay next to each other, talking about their families and their future. For Susan, her future was with him; she knew he felt the same by the way his body responded to her. They kissed on the third date. He waited until she leaned in before he allowed his hands to wander. He waited for her. She felt in control but only to the degree that she could decide when. The how made her shake and sweat in anticipation. He was both dangerous and safe and she held the power to unleash that on her when she was ready.

Marcel's dog, a brindle-coloured boerboel with white chest and black muzzle, raised its head as the couple began to kiss again. It soon settled its oversized head in its speckled paws looking away from its master, always guarding. It was because of Sable that they stayed on the beach, despite the dangers.

The stars moved across the sky, pulling the sun from below the horizon. The two lovers were forced to move when the beach patrol drove along slowly in readiness for the new day. Sable growled as they were given a warning and the vehicle disappeared along the endless beach.

Susan felt Marcel's hand as she put hers in his, fingers interlocking, pulling him to their parked car. She was laughing, sand on the side of her face, her flesh of her legs and arms reacting to the cold by bunching up, creating a goose-flesh appearance. Neither of them wore more than their swimsuits and the blanket over their backs. Sable ran and jumped, pulling on the blanket as if it was a new game.

Twenty-One Years Later...
May 2019
Hampstead, London, UK

Susan shook her head to stop the memories. …

Her hand involuntarily rubbed her neck. The scars remained as the memories faded. Susan hadn't thought about Durban or Marcel in ages. Her subsequent return, recovery, and marriage to Paul pushed those nightmares deep down and into the recesses of her former self. So much so that Paul was unaware of most of what happened. When she woke in a sweat, he would make love to her and tell her that everything was okay. He was safe, secure, and predictable.

Why now? Her feet took her down the familiar pavements of Belsize Square and Hampstead. Her destination was unknown to her. This was her home when she returned nearly two decades ago. This was where, in the Kings Head on a desperate winter's night, she met Candace a year or so after the incident. Candace was fun, witty, and frighteningly smart. Susan smiled fondly as she recalled their first meeting.

Twenty Years Earlier...
February 1999
Hampstead, London, UK

Candace made it her policy to never date a boy for more than three weeks. Susan listened in rapt attention as her new acquaintance espoused her many reasons. Sex was always best in the beginning, she was told; afterwards, it created an inequality. Susan didn't ask how. Men, boys to their core, wanted someone fun and challenging to be around, Candace told her; they didn't want someone smarter than them. If she was to stick around for more than three weeks, they might discover the truth--that she wasn't a bimbo and she didn't want the drama. Susan laughed at that.

When Candace entered a room, all hetero male heads turned. She enjoyed the role she played. The stilettos, worn with jeans or a tight dress, announced her arrival. Her slightly raised chin and proud shoulders announced a confidence that drew out the finest of the male crop for her to examine. Her gratifying genetics did the rest. Slim waist, athletic top with just the right amount of bosom to create mouth-drying curves without the excessiveness of the boob-jobs that many of the girls sported. She was a natural. A beauty. A keeper, as her father might say.

Susan was sitting next to the fire, bundled up with a knitted turtleneck sweater that extended to below her knees and hands above. The sleeves were slightly pushed up to allow her hands out enough to grip a double gin and tonic. The Queen Anne winged chair was large enough for her to curl her legs up and disappear within. The small-ish round wooden table sat between it and another winged chair. It was in this chair that Candace sat down.

"Great spot," she said into the fire. Her hands were outstretched and rubbed together.

"Huh?" Susan wasn't sure who this person was talking to.

"I haven't been here in ages. Forgot about the fireplace. Such a bloody miserable night and thought I'd pop in. Hope you don't mind me talking. Just dumped a bloke and needed some girl time. Sorry, you probably think I'm insane. Just buzzing." Her eyes darted from the fire to Susan to the bar to the door, as if she was expecting someone.

"No, not at all," Susan lied. "Are you okay?"

"Me? Pffff! Never let them see you cry. Not that I'm crying. I'm actually quite pleased with myself."

Susan didn't say anything but raised her eyebrows in reply.

"Matt was a good boy. Probably boyfriend material. Maybe even husband material. Just not for me. Too boring. Too straight. Probably wants me to get knocked up and pump out his 2.1 children while he goes off to work, gets bored of me, screws his secretary, runs off with the nanny, and I'm 45 before you know it. The only screwing I'd get done would be when I managed to get the lid off the peanut butter jar!" She took a large drink from her white wine that Susan just noticed.

"Sounds like you are regretting your decision?"

"Me? No. Maybe a little. He wasn't a bad boy. OK in bed, not great, but a good person. Who knows. What's done is done, eh? Que sera and all that." She stopped her manic monologue and looked at Susan. "Are you okay? If you don't mind me asking, that is?"

Susan took another sip of her drink and placed it down. The fire let out a crackle and a sparkle of red burst briefly above the low flames that licked the logs. "I don't know how I am."

Candace leaned forward with her glass and clinked it against hers. "Honesty. I *fucking* love it. I'm getting some shots. You okay if I order you some? It may help us find out how you are."

Her teeth showed slightly as her mouth curled upwards. She didn't wear a lot of makeup. Just enough to highlight her lips and eyes. Probably a little on her cheeks, again for definition. She got up and her leather jacket dropped to the chair behind her. Her jeans were tight with a studied looseness that screamed athletic body beneath. Her top was tight around the waist and arms, and unbuttoned slightly to show her bra. She was classy, Susan thought. She watched her walk to the bar, place her credit card with the man behind, point to something on the wall, then towards the fireplace. She did a circle in the air with her finger and the bartender smiled and nodded. Then she returned.

"Have one of these; I told handsome to keep them coming at 15 minute intervals. He's cheeky," she looked around and waved to him as she said this. "He'll do in a pinch."

Susan smiled despite herself.

"Listen, sis, I'm not interested in getting to know you or you me. I just need someone who isn't looking to jump me. I need some girl time." Candace knocked a shot back and closed her eyes with a slight wince. Cocking a sideways look at Susan, she added, "I assume I don't need to be concerned?"

"What about?" Then, "No, I mean, no," she stammered when she understood. "I just came here for a quiet drink by myself."

"Are you telling me in a polite way to piss off?"

Susan laughed. "No. You're probably just what I need."

"A fucking tonic, I am." She drank Susan's shot, then turned to the barman and circled her finger in the air. He nodded in understanding.

"Tell me about your guy you dumped," Susan said.

"He's a nobody. Never was somebody. Never will be anybody. But he loved me. I liked him. So I dumped him."

"A bit extreme, don't you think? Perhaps you'd grow to love him?"

"Listen, sis, you need to learn something about men. In aggregate, all men are the same. Individually, you can never tell who are the baddies and who are the goodies. It is a paradox that the whole is predictable while the individual isn't."

"Yeah," Susan said. "Chaos theory, and all that." She lifted her glass and took another sip of her G&T.

Candace stopped short. Sitting back, she rolled up her sleeves to expose a Chanel bracelet, and leaned forward. "You're pretty clever, aren't you?"

Without missing a beat, Susan replied, "And you are bloody brilliant. I'm not fooled by your bluster and drunken act. You were sober when you came over, maybe one drink in; I could tell by your balance on your stilettos. You are hurting and need a friend to drink with. You are assessing me and figured I was as good as any. In fact, you probably wanted to sit next the fireplace and thought I might be some entertainment. Perhaps scare me off."

At that point, the barman placed four shots in between the two women.

Susan picked up a shot and Candace did the same. Neither took their eyes off the other. When the first shot went in, they placed the glass upside down on the tray and immediately picked up the next one. Still saying nothing, they drank it as one, returning the glass to the tray as their bodies shook involuntarily at the roughness of the drink.

Susan's mouth began to twitch. Candace tightened hers in reply. Both eyes flashed and flickered. Then they burst into laughter and spoke at the same time.

"That was one of the best moments of my life," Susan choked through her laughter.

"One of the best. Well played," the other replied. She wiped the whiskey with the back of her hand and turned to the barman. Her finger circled then she shook her head and beckoned him instead. He came.

"I'm not sure what foul stuff we just ingested, but I think it best we change drinks. Do have anything that won't remove our innards completely before the end of the night?"

The barman replied in a Portuguese accent, his handsome face directing his best smile at Candace. "Yes, of course. I'll find something more appropriate."

"Same price?"

"Naturally."

When he left, Candace winked at Susan. "Definitely, a candidate."

"Sorry for that. I don't know what came over me. I am not generally that blunt. You must have brought it out in me."

"Never be sorry. Us woman have enough shit thrown at us. Being sorry is for everyone else. You've got a brain. You're obviously gorgeous, even if you don't feel it right now. What happened? If you don't mind me asking?"

"I don't know what I mind. I'm just numb. I probably need a friend more than you do."

"Consider it done. Candace's my name. Candace Williams."

"Susan Leigh. Nice to meet you."

"Likewise."

"What do you do when you are not dumping marrying types or invading the space of people next to fires?"

"Not much, to tell you the truth. I am just finishing off my degree and then I'll see."

"What you are studying?"

"Medicine. I don't like to say it in case it scares off the boys. Intimidation and all that, you know."

Susan nodded. "The only thing worse than a beautiful woman is a beautiful woman with a brain. Scares the hell out of everyone. It is as though all the doors open up and we can sleep our way through any problem our brain can't solve."

"Got it in one. Why do we care? And why have you left that fine specimen at the bar unattended? My god, the more I drink, the better he is." Candace shook her head in mock sincerity.

"He's okay. Before the booze, he was around an eight; now, he is closing in on ten. I agree. As long as he doesn't open his mouth."

"Put a sock in it and just get on with it, I always say. Have you heard Beckham speak? He should keep his skills on the field where he should be. That, and taking his shirt off. I'm not a footie fan, but I'd watch that all day long."

"You do say whatever comes into your mind, don't you?"

"What's the point keeping it in? Maybe if I'd sing, they'd let me into a girl band and I'd be married to him instead of Posh."

"They still together?"

"The Beckhams or Spice Girls?"

"The band."

"Who cares? Now, tell me about why you are sitting alone here instead of with Mr. Ten over there."

Susan's hand went to her neck and rubbed it. Her hair fell alongside her shoulder and down her front. She hadn't cut it since South Africa. Since Marcel. Since that night.

"Just a guy I knew. We were supposed to married by now."

"Piece of shit," Candace interjected. "What did he do to you? I hate him already."

Susan swallowed. All her body hurt, despite the shots. Her elbow twitched and her shoulders turned in. She writhed as though waking from a long sleep and her body needed to move. Her head began to shake left and right as though the act would make what she would say less true.

"He died."

Chapter Two

Hampstead, UK (February 1999)

"Oh my god. I'm sorry," Candace said quickly. "I'm such an ass, you know."

"It's okay," Susan said quietly. "It's probably time."

Candace said nothing. Her hands made her way to Susan's and held them tight.

"All I have to remember from him is this scar." She lifted her hair and lowered the turtleneck.

Candace put her hand to her mouth and recoiled. Susan felt her new friend's fingertips lightly brush the pink and white scar tissue of something that circled right around. She guessed that Candace had a million questions. None passed her lips. She waited for Susan's story at her own time.

Susan nodded as another round of drinks were placed in between them. Shots, a half bottle of Port and a selection of cheese and crackers. Mr. Ten was doing all he could to impress. This time, neither noticed.

"It was a year ago, a lifetime ago. Before…" she trailed off and put her hand to her mouth as she closed her eyes. A single tear began to escape and she quickly wiped it away. "I moved to South Africa with a man I knew would be the father of my children. My god, he made me shake when he was near me." Her face softened at the memory. "When he said he needed to return to his home, I thought my life was over. Then he asked me to join him and I knew everything would be okay. Even my parents loved him. He was a giver. If he had ten pounds to his name and you needed it, he'd give you it without even letting you know how much it was to him."

Candace nodded and moved closer, taking Susan's hands in hers again.

"The day itself was more perfect than I could have imagined. It was natural. Neither of us wanted it to end. So we didn't move. We stayed on that beach overnight. When we got home, we shared a hot shower, made love and slept until noon. The balcony doors in our bedroom were open. I will always remember how the sound of the waves crashing comforted me." Susan's fingers circled the wine glass, now half full of Port.

"At some point, our eyes opened and he went to make us some coffee and let the dog outside. I didn't hear anything for quite a while so I decided to see what was keeping him." Susan paused, eyes closed, and inhaled deeply before continuing. "When I saw him, his face fell. As if everything he had been doing was wasted." Susan paused again, trying to keep the dialogue flowing against the emotion that welled inside her. "The captors followed his gaze and saw me in an instant. They looked like hyenas to me."

"Captors?" Candace exclaimed. She quieted herself and let the story continue.

"I don't know what you know about Durban, Umhlanga and South Africa, but it is not all Kumbaya. I don't know much about the local black population but the Afrikaans and other whites tend to keep to themselves. Communities are protected by signs warning of armed response and high solid fences/walls surrounding each home. Once inside, it is charming and warm and wonderful." Susan allowed herself an involuntary smile as the image of what life was like with Marcel washed over her. "Outside is seen to be dangerous and vulnerable. Each family scoffs at the danger but you won't see them in the black areas—especially at night. Life consists of moving from one 'safe' bubble to another, preferably by car. Despite this heightened level of security, you feel safe. Wine flows, conversation ranges from whatever you can think of to things you can't. It is a great world. You hear of home invasions, robberies, terrible crimes but it is always somewhere else. Someone else."

"Why go there if it is so dangerous?" Candace asked, eyes wide, alcohol forgotten.

"Because Marcel was there. I would go to hell and back for him. I loved him completely."

Candace nodded. She poured some more Port into Susan's glass. They both drank silently for a moment, absorbing the scene that had been painted. She didn't want to prod but wanted her to continue about her captors. Susan sensed that the pause was sufficient and continued with her story.

"The wall safe was open and the picture in front thrown next to the patio doors. Sable was going crazy outside, smashing against the door, white saliva foaming into strings that splattered the glass door, her body and the floor around her. Their eyes followed mine to the dog, then to Marcel. He was tied up with his hands behind him. One of his legs was bent the wrong way. I don't know how he managed to keep quiet through that. I guess he was hoping they wouldn't discover me." Susan's voice was distant, as if recalling a movie and not her actual life. "Are you sure you want to hear this?"

Candace nodded and poured some more Port for herself. Susan had barely touched hers.

"I watched, frozen, as the bigger of the two walked calmly to me... 'You're a pretty one. Your boy has been brave. I can see why.' He took a knife and allowed the blade to trace my body." Susan paused briefly, shaking slightly at the memory. "It barely touched me. I didn't flinch. I was... I was struck dumb and mute, staring at Marcel, hoping that he had a solution. Hoping that he triggered a hidden alarm. Hoping that this was a nightmare and I would wake shortly."

"There was no talking. We knew how royally fucked we were and that it was best to accept the inevitable. I waited for talk of ransom, for reasons, "why us?" I thought maybe Marcel was a secret agent and they were from the government, looking to extract secrets. … Nothing. Just a bloody fucking robbery. … They thought we were out working. … They must have broken in while we were fast asleep. … They couldn't open the safe, so they got Marcel to do it when he got up to get me coffee and breakfast."

Susan put her head down. "I don't think I can go on." She started to cry gently but quickly stopped. "No. I will tell you, if only so those bastards don't take over my life."

Candace said nothing. She sat bolt upright at the edge of her chair, ignoring Mr. Ten's clearing of the next table or the tears that were creating mascara tracks on her own face. Her hand was firmly over her mouth.

"The big guy motioned me back to the bedroom. He was rough. He made me bleed. He threatened to cut me open if I didn't do what he wanted. I did. … Then the other one came and dropped his trousers. He couldn't get it up and beat me instead. … I took the blows to the head, feeling the impact of his fist like an operation under local anaesthetic. I knew it was happening by the tugs and blows, but felt nothing apart from the movement of the rest of my body. …" Susan took a break with her eyes closed, breathing deeply and exhaling, before continuing. "He then used his hand on me. It was small enough to fit inside. … He didn't stop until he was hard enough to stick his cock in me. He smashed his bony hips against mine, slapping my thighs vigorously with his until he slowed, seized up, and exhaled as he pumped his seed into me. … His breath stank of weed and tobacco." Susan's face wrinkled at the memory of the stench. "His lips curled back to show yellow pegs where his teeth should have been. He yelled like a savage as he licked me with his filthy tongue, biting my breasts in turn until they bled."

Susan's fingers trembled and found the Port, downing it in one gulp. Her body shook and her eyes stared blankly into the distance, glassy and unwilling to shed further tears.

"When the little one left the room, I heard screams from Marcel. I couldn't imagine what they were doing to him. I cried out. The little one returned with a rope. … One of those that you see on an old boat. Heavy and scratchy. He put it around my neck, tightened it, and dragged me out of the room." Her voice dropped as her body re-lived the spoken words. "I was naked, bleeding, and broken. I just wanted them to kill me. Instead, they stood me next to the lounge door and strung the rope over the door, tying it in such a way so as to ensure I stood on my tip toes if I wanted to breathe. In front of me, they put Marcel, now naked on the floor. They tied him up like a hog before a butchering."

Candace shook with adrenaline and horror. She became hyper-aware of everyone in the pub, watching with wariness any person who approached. She found herself clutching her elbows, arms crossed in front of her chest, legs tightly shut at the knees.

"I heard the large one disappear into our kitchen and return with the meat cleaver. I remember laughing at such a ridiculous utensil until I saw how Marcel was able to break joints of meat in readiness for the braai. The big one wielded this with an evil smile towards the little one. I couldn't hear anything as everything went silent. No dog barking in the background. No laughing. Just a high pitched sound in my ears as I watched my Marcel, bent over, and unware of what was coming his way."

"They taunted him. They asked him to call them *Kefers*. They kicked him in the ribs each time they repeated that word. As the little one kicked him, the big one came down with all his might on Marcel's…"

Susan's voice choked and the tears ran down her cheeks. Apart from that, there was no emotion on her face. A vacant look filled her eyes as her head moved down and to her left as her cheek touched her shoulder in a tender pain. Her eyes closed and her breathing became deep, like in sleep, and her body slumped. When she looked up at Candace, she was back in the pub.

"It was horrible," she whispered hoarsely. "The blood, the sound Marcel, my beautiful Marcel. Oh, my god, how I loved him. He was so brave. For me, I know. All for me. The two of them were hypnotised with the killing of my love. It drove them mad. They took turns. Taking their anger against all white men on my poor, beautiful, Marcel."

Candace could not control her anxiety any longer. "How did you survive this? You were tied up. They were armed. There were two of them."

Susan looked at her new friend dead in the eye and smiled. "Well, that was true." She swallowed her tears as her voice shook from the adrenaline of reliving that day. "But I had Sable. And they just killed her master." What started as little more than an intense whisper returned to her normal voice. "I wasn't dying and I wasn't imagining the silence. Sable stopped barking because she had moved from the back glass door around the house to our bedroom. There, she came in through the open patio doors and ran at full speed. She hit the larger guy first. He was taking his turn with the cleaver. She was fast, vicious, and efficient. All sixty kilograms of prime dog muscle slammed into this animal man and knocked him over. Sable's jaws went for his throat and closed." Susan wiped the tears with the back of her hand defiantly. "Her head shook violently three or four times and I saw what must have been the remains of his windpipe hanging between her jaws and his still body as she turned to look at the smaller one. He was frozen in the way I had been earlier. Sable didn't hesitate. She sprang on him, knocked him over and her jaws tore into the side of his neck. She shook and held on despite the flaying of his legs until I heard the distinct sounds of bones snapping and her jaws closed. Her body seemed twice its size, bolstered by adrenaline and rage. She went back to the larger man and nudged his head as if to check if he was alive. Nothing. She did the same with the smaller man. Nothing. She glanced at me and then went to Marcel." When she finished, Susan bit down on both lips and closed her eyes. Her mouth had to open as her breathing was now fast. Reliving this memory hurt and her body was exhausted.

Susan's voice expressed the love and gratitude at the majesty of Sable's power. All its breeding for that one moment. Candace remained silent.

"If there was one creature on earth capable of loving Marcel more than either me or his mother, it was Sable. She cried and tried to lick the oozing blood off his face. I saw, I think I saw, his eyes flicker open to see me one last time. I believe that he smiled as if he knew I was safe. But I can't trust my memory on that point. It was so intense. So surreal. I tiptoed and tugged the rope gingerly as I coaxed it along the top of the door to the edge where it slackened and I could relax. Sable came over to me and licked my face and muzzled me gently as if to say I was safe. I blacked out and the next thing I remember was paramedics taking me in an ambulance."

Susan stopped, wiped her face and nose with the back of her sleeve and drank three shots in quick succession followed by the port. Candace matched her in silence.

"Holy shit," Candace said. "What happened to the dog?"

"I brought her with me when I returned to the UK."

"And Marcel?"

"I buried him in his family's plot in Pretoria. His parents were so supportive and lovely. I couldn't ask for better people. But I couldn't stay in that country. Such a beautiful country. I want to understand. My mind does understand the hatred the blacks have towards the whites. I was later told that these men were not local—apparently, the local Zulus and other local tribes were not known to conduct themselves like this. It was probably some immigrants from other parts of Africa who look upon Johannesburg as the New York of Africa. They probably couldn't make it there so they took to looting elsewhere. Crime has become a major problem. But my heart could not let me stay there. Everything reminded me of him."

"Do you have any friends you can be with?"

"Other than you?"

Candace almost cried. She had just met Susan. "Anyone you can stay with tonight? You can't be alone."

"I have Sable. I'll be safe."

"Yes, but you need more than being safe from fear. You need to be free to be safe and try to find happiness. Failing that, contentment."

"You're a good person, Candace."

"Then you'll stay with me. I live at home but there is plenty of space. I'm just up a few blocks from here." She got up to stand but her legs were a little weak. "On second thought, let's call a cab."

"I need to go home to Sable. She has to be let out."

"Can I meet her?"

Susan hesitated. "Sure. But she is quite particular about people and is very protective. Don't hand me anything or raise your voice around me."

"After what you just told me, I will give her space and let her come to me on her terms in her time."

"Perfect. We'll just be half an hour with her and then we'll go to yours, if you still want to?"

"Sounds like a plan." Candace finished her Port and went to pay the bill. Part of her wondered if it was such a good idea to be near such a damaged person. Then Mr. Ten appeared and she thought that it was no more dangerous than some of the men she went home with. *There but for the grace of God go I,* she muttered to herself as the cab arrived.

Chapter 3

Hampstead, London (February 1999)

Susan's eyes opened to an unfamiliar warmth, a different pillow than her own, and a dull ache from the night before. Her shoes were off, but she was still in her clothes. Her hands felt the corduroy ridges of the sofa beneath cotton sheets. The duvet smelled of faint perfume, or possibly lavender. She couldn't trust her senses yet. She coughed, involuntarily trying to remove the smoke of the fire and pub from the night before. She swung her legs onto the floor and sat up, holding her head. Her hair covered her hands and nearly touched the floor as her elbows planted themselves on her knees.

The silence was broken ever so gently by the occasional sound of water gurgling through the radiators. The ceilings were high with the expected Victorian detail on the coving and fringes around the windows. The floor was carpeted. The room's door was closed with a key on the inside still in the lock. A large television sat on an antique-looking side table. Books filled shelves, and pillows were everywhere.

A smile crept onto her face as her memory returned. A rough night of memories. A new friend. Anxiety suddenly gripped her as she looked at the time. Sable would need her. The late night/early morning visit went well but dogs needed walks.

She got up and wondered if it would be okay to just leave. She glanced at a mirror and fixed herself before opening the door. She could smell something being cooked. The aroma of coffee and sounds of conversation increased as she reached the last steps of the staircase.

"Everyone, this is Susan. Susan, everyone." Candace swept her hand over the faces that looked at her guest. Susan wasn't prepared for a full house. She had been hoping to slip away quietly.

"Uh, hi?" She smiled and shrugged, then rubbed her neck and opened her hair so that it covered the scars.

"Nice to meet you, Susan." Candace's mother, Rose, came close and hugged her gently, with a little extra squeeze for good measure. "Can I get you something? Water, tea?"

"Hot Chocolate?" Candace added. She handed Susan one and sat down nearest the Aga. Susan followed and hovered next to her.

"You look like a sensible girl, Susan," Rose said amiably. "Can you tell me how I have four beautiful and intelligent girls and not one marriage proposal? Look at them. Aren't they the picture of health?"

Susan dropped her eyes, embarrassed. "I can't say for certain, Ma'am…"

"Stop that nonsense. I'm Rose. Now, continue."

"Uh, ok. I just think that maybe women don't need to get married." Her voice was uncharacteristically quiet. Respectful, bordering on shy.

"Do you need to get married?" Rose countered, good naturedly, then shifted as though a thought slammed into her. "I'm sorry. That was insensitive."

Susan shot a look at Candace who shrugged her shoulders. There was so much love in the room that Susan didn't mind. "I would marry for true love," she said after a slightly longer pause than intended.

"See, girls? True love. Maybe you can learn something from Candace's new friend. Eminently sensible."

"I, for one, haven't found Mr. Right yet," Candace said as her mug clunked against the marble countertop. The kitchen had a large marble island where the family congregated. The breakfast table was round, wooden, and set into a bay window to afford the best morning light for reading newspapers, drinking coffee, and crunching on crispy bacon.

"Don't look at me," Mary said. "I'm too young to even be thinking of this stuff."

"If you don't think about life, it will happen to you regardless," said Elizabeth. "Think about it thoroughly and then reject it out of hand." She smiled and nodded to her father, Jim, who sipped his morning coffee and knew better than to contribute to certain topics.

"I would love to get married, Mum, but I am concerned that you'll kick me out of the house. Where would I get such service elsewhere? Do you think my husband would wash my clothes and cook dinner?" Samantha delivered the message all the daughters concluded long ago. There was no better living arrangement than home. No expenses meant more going out money. More clothes. More options. Freedom that included renting a flat meant enslavement and a serious reduction of their quality of life. Besides, she already had a marriage proposal by Tom. They called off the wedding at the last minute. She told her family that it was second thoughts. She had not shared the real reason yet.

"I'm sure your father would be happy to have your husbands move in here," Rose said with a smile, knowing the answer.

"Hmmm…." Jim mumbled, knowing that there was no correct answer in the circumstance. He would have been content to have everyone live at their home. It was large enough, purchased at the depths of a housing cycle just as his banking career was taking off. The idea of having some additional male opinions to counter his four daughters and wife was appealing.

"There's always Tom," Samantha said, a little too softly.

All eyes turned to her.

"Tell us!" Elizabeth purred.

"Nothing to tell. You all know him. He's my tall, dark, handsome man. He's polite, dresses well and makes me feel fantastic."

"But I thought that was over?" Rose said with a smile, filling the room.

"I think that calls for a toast!" Candace said.

There was a general chorus of approval and Susan lifted her hot chocolate and touched its sides with those within reach.

∞

Visits became more frequent and even Sable was allowed to visit to give her approval. She did. Sable was happy to curl up next to the Aga or in the garden during one of the Williams' weekly BBQs. Wine always flowed freely.

Susan shuddered as the memories flowed through her. Her feet continued on the pavement, aimlessly taking her anywhere but home. She remembered embracing the bottle, the bonhomie, the network of Williams' friends, the weddings of Samantha, the whirlwind of Rose's past, the Nazi gold, Rhona and, of course, Candace and Pepe. None of the memories was more painful than the one that eventually led her to marrying Paul.

"Let me ask you a question," Jim said, looking at her in her tight dress, mascara'd eyes, and perfume that she knew even he would find irresistible. "Which is the real you? Sober Susan or Drunk Susan?"

"I don't know," she said with a small voice. "I fear I am no longer relevant." Her shoulders lifted like a little girl's and added, "I tried to kill myself, did you know that?"

Jim closed his eyes and shook his head. "No." He didn't offer any further conversation. Instead, he slowly turned the wheel of the Range Rover Vogue and manoeuvred out of the hotel's underground parking. It was past midnight and the roads had remnants of the revellers staggering home from the pubs.

Susan pulled her seatbelt on across her top. Her dress was short and her bare legs were cold. It reminded her of that day in South Africa with Marcus after the beach. The gooseflesh. Her hands began to shake as she reached for the heating. She turned it up to 28 Celsius and turned the seat heater on full. They didn't talk. She had called Jim the way she would her father, if he was still alive. He always came, despite the hour or locale. She looked out the window at the humanity crawling home at the end of a long day. The car glided effortless down Park Lane, Hyde Park being closed at that time of the night. As it made its way through Marble Arch and Edgeware, she froze and her hand involuntarily grabbed Jim's arm.

He looked sideways at her. "Everything OK?"

She didn't answer him. She was staring at two men. One, very large and the other smaller. They were dark skinned, hard to determine their origin. They walked casually on the pavement, sharing a laugh and gesturing at girls as they passed. When they saw Susan, they waved and smiled and walked on.

Her reaction was immediate. Marcel was on the floor, being broken by those two thugs. She had just been brutally raped by both men, but especially the small one. The one who couldn't get it up. The one who dragged her back to watch Marcel's demise with a rope around her neck. Who strung her up on the door, naked and bleeding. Who waved at her and then smiled before raising his arms for the final time against her Marcel. Susan shook and grabbed for Jim's hand. He let her have it. She curled up as much as her seatbelt allowed her before letting out a small cry and buried her head in Jim's arm. He slowed but didn't stop.

"What's going on, Susan?" His voice was low. Concerned.

She couldn't talk. Her other hand covered her mouth and tears began to rain from her eyes. She gripped Jim's hand with surprising strength and then sat bolt upright in her chair, bringing his hand over to her side.

Jim was forced to grip her hand to give support to her strength.

Her body convulsed despite her attempts to control herself. She grabbed his hand with her other hand so that both of her hands were holding onto him. Jim silently drove the car down the nearly deserted road in autopilot. They were still at least ten minutes from home.

Susan bit her lips and plunged her hands between her legs, still holding onto Jim's hand. He felt the hard, young muscle of her bare leg and barely registered where his hand was.

"It's okay, sweetheart. Everything's fine," he said.

She pushed his hand against her. He didn't remove it.

They drove in silence for a few minutes.

"You're safe, Susan. You're okay. Everything is fine." Jim knew everything wasn't fine. She was rubbing his hand against herself and gripping his hand as though her life depended on it. He felt his adrenaline begin to flow and his heartrate increase. Part of him was being turned on by this in a big way.

She sat in stony silence, rubbing his hand with her fingers and rubbing his hand against her. She opened his hand and put his fingers against her, always pulling his fingers and hand towards her. He could feel that she wasn't wearing anything under her dress.

He let her, while keeping his eyes on the road.

"It's okay, sweetheart," he repeated. "Everything is okay."

She stopped shaking and the tears flowed less violently, but still gripped his hand against her. "This is very inappropriate," she managed.

Jim pulled the car over and turned to look at her. "Nothing is inappropriate if this is what you need."

She stared at him, uncertain what he meant her to do. He was the only man apart from Marcel whom she respected and loved. Yes, truly loved. As a daughter, her father. But also as a woman, a man. She held his hand firmly where it was. He did nothing either way apart from looking directly at her. She stared back in wild uncertainty as if seeing him for the first time.

He pulled back into traffic, hand still between her legs, and continued to drive back to his home where she assumed she was still welcome to stay in the guest room. Or would he share that with her as well? Her head spun with the permutations. Would he throw all he had with Rose away for her? For this? Her body yearned for him even more. There was a heat between her legs that she hadn't felt since Marcel. Her chest rose and fell as her body tried to regulate the intensity of her feelings.

They reached the circular pebble drive that crunched under the weight of the Range Rover's tyres. Jim put the car in park and turned off the engine. His hand was still firmly between her legs and she was looking at him with unmistakeably desire.

Jim undid his seatbelt with his free hand and gently pulled his left hand free from hers. She sat stock still in her seat as he exited the vehicle and came around to her door.

He opened her door and leaned across to undo her seatbelt. She slid her legs to the side and stepped out of the car, using the car's step and his hand as a support. He closed the door and the two stood facing each other.

"Susan, I will shake your hand instead of giving you a hug." He was rubbing her hand as he spoke. She held his two hands with hers.

"I don't know what I'm doing," she said, her eyes open and large as they searched his face.

"None of us know what we are doing. Just know that you are loved and cared by many people. I don't want to hear that you are trying to kill yourself. If you need to talk, anytime, day or night, you call me or Rose. OK? You understand?"

Susan began to understand. Her body wanted to hold him and make love to him and dream of him caring for her the way he cared for Rose and Candace, Elizabeth, Mary, and Samantha. She loved his hands in hers and didn't want to let go. She began to nod her head in acknowledgement to her conversation with herself. Her eyes glittered with a film that refused to fall. Her hands began to shake slightly as she pulled them out of his.

"Your actions," she said, "are the kindest thing anyone has ever done to me. You treated me like a person in need instead of the slut that I have become."

Jim's eyes softened and his face became heavy with thought and emotion. "You are not a slut, Susan. You are a powerful, intelligent, and wonderful woman. I wish that one day you will see what all of us know about you."

He took a step backwards, partly in fear of what he might do or they might do. He was aware of how charged the environment was. How much his body wanted to make love to a desperate, beautiful woman who was sorely in need of a father figure. He wasn't stupid. And he knew he should have removed his hand sooner, but part of him wanted it. Needed it. His body shook from the desire to take her. He bowed and indicated her to walk before him to the door.

Susan held her two fingers against her lips, kissing them the way she wished she was kissing Jim. She blew the kisses to him and disappeared inside the door. She made her way upstairs and the thought crossed her mind that she would still see him later that night but dismissed it when she saw the warm glow of light in Rose's room as she waited for her husband.

Outside, Jim collapsed against his vehicle, reliving the sensation of her skin against his hand and those intense unending minutes of his hand between her legs and, briefly, of his fingers touching… he shook his head to remove the image. He looked up and saw the nightlight of Rose waiting for him. He took in some deep breaths of night air before locking his car and going inside.

The next morning, Jim was polite and never spoke of the incident again—to Susan or Rose or even himself.

A month later, Susan met Paul. They were married within six months.

Chapter 4

Twenty Years Later… May 2019 Hampstead, London

The past belonged to the past, she said to herself as she walked beyond the Kings Head and the memories of her meeting Candace. Thoughts of Sable filled her head and she felt her eyes water at the manifestation of love incarnate in the form of the dog who saved her life. It was Sable who approved of Paul and welcomed him into their circle. Candace also approved but she had already met her Pepe and was swept off to Argentina and back again and anywhere else Royals played polo and Pepe could sell his world class ponies. Her feet led her past her good friend's family home, snugly secure behind their wrought-iron gates. It was hard to imagine such a serene setting for a drama that Candace's family lived out nearly twenty years earlier. Nazi gold, horrific grandparents and imposters. Yet she and her family had found peace.

Her hand touched the space between her breasts and rubbed it. Marcel loved that spot. He would lay his head on her and breathe her in, and she him. Paul, on the other hand, hadn't noticed her in years. He had been so perfect. So calm. So steady. Maybe it was her inability to share everything, like the way she could with Candace. She told him about the attack, but never went into details.

Paul was a good man, she thought, as the pavement passed beneath her. Hampstead Heath, Redington Road, the quiet soothing of affluence encased in brick and surrounded by greenery. Her mind kept returning to Marcel. Then Candace and that uncharacteristic opening by her of her wounds to a total stranger. Perhaps that is how it had to be. If she had known Candace for longer than a day, it would have been too difficult, too strange, too painful.

Susan walked in contemplative silence, head tilted down, without direction. She had told Paul that she had an appointment in London. There was none. She couldn't bear to be in his vicinity when he visited his whore. How he didn't know that she knew was beyond her. A woman knows. It made her feel, she didn't know how it made her feel. That was the problem. She should be enraged, smashing things, smashing him. Instead, she shrugged it off and accepted the new reality.

She stopped in realisation.

She didn't love Paul. That had been obvious for a while. But, she never loved him. Perhaps the marriage, the safety, the big dreams were just part of the salve needed to recover from Marcel. *Bloody hell*, she thought. *Eighteen years is one bloody long time to recover.*

Her body as much as her lungs sighed. Her shoulders drooped while keeping erect. Her posture was always perfect. Her foot slid on some ice cream dropped by an unseen child.

"Shit," she muttered to herself. She looked down, then caught sight of the man from the breakfast café. She felt something warm in her chest and checked herself. He barely noticed her earlier, preferring to scribble madly in a notebook instead. He was walking straight towards her.

"Made or produced?" he asked with a smile on his face.

"Pardon?" her mind tried to understand what she missed in his sentence.

"Was it made by someone or excreted by something? Sorry, it sounded so much more eloquent in my mind."

"Uh, ha," she managed as she scraped her sole against adjoining grass. "Not excreted by man or beast. Not sure which I prefer."

"Depends," he said good-naturedly. "But I think they are pretty equally nasty."

"You're the guy from the café," she said, ignoring his remark and changing subjects.

"Yeah. And you're the gal from the same café. Sorry I wasn't more talkative. You caught me in a moment."

"It was refreshing."

His eyebrow rose. "Really? What are your usual experiences?" His voice was part mock, part interest.

"Apart from the visual undressing, general misogynistic paternalism?"

"Naturally. That goes without saying." He was grinning now.

"Pretty much as it went today. To tell you the truth, it made me feel old." She couldn't believe she said the words. What was she doing, she thought? Flirting like a schoolgirl?

"If you're fishing for compliments, I'm happy to oblige. But I won't insult you with any line."

Susan looked at his hair which was longer than it should have been for his age, with the hints of grey that would, in time, make him look very distinguished. His face was tanned, and his body athletic. She could tell by the way he sat and confirmed it when she saw him walking towards her. His shoulders were broad, like a rower's. His teeth, white and straight. He looked like an athletic, non-smoking Marlborough Man. She locked her eyes with his, not flinching as his head moved while his eyes remained fixed on hers. Grey-blue eyes that hinted at intelligence with its twinkle. He waited as she calculated internally.

"I'm married," she said, finally.

"Of course you are."

"So there's nothing that can happen between us."

"I only said that you are someone I'd like to get to know. If you're not interested, I'll be on my way. Life's too short to be afraid." He started walking.

"I am afraid."

Her words stopped him. He turned, slowly, and extended his hand. "My name's Romeo. I'm also terrified. Nice to meet someone with some honesty."

"Susan. Nice name. I guess you get a lot of ribbing for it."

"No idea what you're talking about," he said, grinning again. "Perhaps you can fill me in?"

"When?"

"How about now? I'll walk with you until you get where you need to go. You'll know by then whether you want to know more or see me at all."

Susan knew already, but played along. They started walking in the direction of the Heath, then through it and past the Royal Free and up towards Haverstock Hill. They turned right on All England's Lane.

Susan didn't have a destination. She had already visited Sable's memorial plaque where she was buried. Candace was away and she couldn't bear the thought of returning home to Paul. Or his damn brother if he actually arrived as he said he would.

Romeo put his hands in his jacket to keep Susan at ease. He barely noticed the Hull shotgun shell with the depressed primer.

Chapter 5

The Shotgun Shell

Romeo had placed the end of the barrel in his mouth. It still had residue of gun oil on it. A bead of sweat crossed his forehead and onto his nose. It joined tears that began to flow.

His hand reached for the trigger.

It was a bit of a stretch. The stock was on the floor. He, on the edge of the bed. Leaning over the gun.

His index finger toyed with the engraved trigger. His palm was stretched away from him and the stretch was beginning to burn. It was the moment of truth.

He closed his eyes and waited. His muscles refused to respond.

He pushed hard against the trigger and felt it move. His body shook with adrenaline.

Click.

He shook harder, then dropped the gun to the floor. His hand fell beside him, slick with sweat. Was he dead?

His head bobbled as it strained to understand. Then, he vomited.

He curled himself into a ball and began to rock fast, then slow.

His eyes were twitching in fast motion behind eyelids that flashed with light and back.

He couldn't stop shaking. His body was wet from head to toe. He was afraid to look to see if he had wet himself. He knew he hadn't shat himself. That was something.

It was either two minutes or two hours, he couldn't decide. He opened his eyes to see the shotgun lying next to him. He rolled onto his stomach, then arms and knees and crawled to look at it. His fingers effortlessly flipped the latch and the over-under cracked open with a smooth movement. The single cartridge was automatically expelled and he instinctively moved his head sideways to avoid the shell. Always maintained. He couldn't remember the last time it misfired.

He looked at the remaining shell. It remained in place like a soldier awaiting orders. Nothing wrong there.

He pulled the covers off the bed to get to the space under it where the flying shotgun shell lay. He picked it up and examined it. The plastic casing with Hull written across it. The brass-plated steel that gave it a very classy look. It was perfect and unharmed. He turned it over in his right hand and looked at the primer, sitting proudly at the end and center of the brass. There was the unmistakeable dimple of the firing pin that had struck it.

Holding it carefully, he placed it on the side table next to his bed. Pulled back the covers. Slid in and went to sleep. The shower sounded like a distant rain falling.

He awoke six hours later, turned off the shower, and put away his gun.

The house was quiet. He was alone. No one would have known for weeks.

He dressed in light tanned trousers with an expensive blue shirt that was understated in every way but price covered by a navy blazer. Shoes, Church's. Socks, a gift from his ex. She always had great taste.

The door closed behind him and the world was alive. Spring blossoms. Black dog, red lead. Men, women, children. Even the piercing sound of an ambulance on its way to the Royal Free, blue lights vibrant in the new air.

Grey and brown pebbles on the tarmac under his shoes. Diesel fumes, pollen, and greenish dog shit. The present made real through memory. He was alive.

His fingers felt the stolid cylinder with the depressed primer in his pocket. It reminded him that he was either dead already and all of this was a dream or nothing really mattered after all. He could fight back on his terms.

His lips began to murmur as he walked. His stride increased. He crossed into Hampstead Heath. His lips began to pass sounds. No one was listening. No one was ever listening, he thought.

"Screw 'em," he said out loud. He turned his head to see if anyone even noticed. None did.

"Screw. You!" he yelled at the top of his lungs. His face turned red as he exhaled the words. Veins became visible on his neck and forehead. He was doubled over when he finished. This time, people noticed. When he caught their eyes, they quickly looked away and kept walking.

His fingers turned the Hull cartridge and he felt like smiling for the first time in as long a time as he could remember.

Inspiration

Time was late. Traffic, light. Sky, dark.

The intense aroma of coffee mixed with chocolate on his palate kept Romeo awake and filled the car. The road stretched in front, dry and inviting. It was the perfect drive.

Air began to buffet Romeo's ears as he opened the window. To stop the pounding, he opened the passenger side window a crack. The wind, cool with a hint of herbicide from the neighboring fields washed his face and mind clear. To his left, an empty seat apart from a box.

"She loves me," he said to himself as his hand gingerly picked a handful of the box's contents and threw it out the window.

"She loves me not," he said again, tossing a second handful out the window.

"She loves me." Another handful.

"She loves me not." Another again.

To the sound of Smooth Radio, playing Billy Joel, the box emptied through the window, into the whistling darkness, onto the road behind.

His hometown in mid-West United States was a distant point of departure, the place he told himself he would never return to—in time or place. London and his new life lay ahead.

January, 2019
M40 Motorway, UK

On his way from Birmingham to London, Romeo absent-mindedly began throwing all elements of his life out of his moving car window. His Range Rover carried the materials his builder requested to finalise his new kitchen along with boxes of screws for the new addition. Not all at once, but slowly. A post-flower world where screws were petals and his heart bled pain felt by his namesake. He drove almost thirty minutes at highway speed as the contents of the boxes slowly emptied onto the motorway behind him. He stopped at the side of the road and threw the kitchen carcasses onto the hard shoulder. He would not have dreamed of throwing those on the road, at least not yet.

When he reached London, he drove as if in a trance to his Hampstead home. The gate slid sideways along its track to allow him in and closed just as silently. The brick was lit in a soft glow of yellow light, a security feature that seemed to work more effectively than the CCTV cameras that captured every movement on the manicured garden. Inside, he turned on the television, opened a bottle of Guatemalan spiced sipping rum and fell asleep to the sounds of the History channel.

The morning news talked about road closures and countless road traffic accidents along the M40. None of this would have made headlines if it wasn't for the odd coincidence that the Minister of State for Housing managed to get three flat tyres on her journey from Birmingham back to London. Headlines reflecting her pneumatically challenged tyres to her flat policy on housing were inevitable. The newscasters also mentioned that a large number of incidents were reported along that stretch of the M40. There was no further news on the matter.

And in that moment grew the seed that manifested his frustrations against the world, society, and himself. He realized that anyone could impact the whole with a very minimum of effort.

And it all came down to the humble black screw used by every builder on every continent. Designed to screw plasterboard to studs, it came in various sizes. Most importantly, it was ubiquitous, cheap and anonymous. Anyone could buy it.

Its main quality: the surprising ease by which it attached itself to tyres. Soft enough to be picked up, twisted and pushed by use into the tyre. The breach would cause the tyre to empty itself of air. Sometimes slowly. Sometimes violently. Mostly, a controlled loss with the aim being to disable and inconvenience cars, trucks and users of the road network. And after that? Something would present itself. Screws would never be enough to jolt the world aright.

It was like inducing a heart attack in a person to force him to lose weight and change his lifestyle.

Malicious litter was and could only be the beginning. The objective was to get the masses to engage. To break free from the apathy of play station appeasement, vicarious joy through spectator sport, and the comfort provided the 99 percent by the 1 percent.

Chapter 7

Four Months Later… Belsize Park, London (May, 2019)

Breakfast consisted of a Full English at Oliver's. He ate alone. His moleskin diary sat open next to him. His mind raced through subjects and targets. Ways in which he could impact. Shake from slumber the numbed masses. As he wrote, he felt a throbbing behind his right ear. The tension rose within him. It was almost unbearable.

"But that is why I must bear it," he said to himself, chin tucked tight into his chest. His hands wrote in scrawls on both sides of the paper. The ink of his uni-ball pen seeped through in points.

"Excuse me?" A voice beside him said.

"Sorry?" Romeo replied.

"Did you ask me something?" Her eyebrows were raised, face open, and eyes looking right into him.

"Nope. I must have been mumbling to myself. I get carried away." He sheepishly grinned and put his hands under the table when he realised that he had both ink and egg yolk on them.

"Sorry. Didn't mean to intrude." She put her head down, allowing some of her hair to loosen and fall astride her face. "Are you a writer?" The last word brought her eyes to his again, but her head remained bent downwards.

Very Diana, thought Romeo as he reddened slightly. "No, just thinking and putting down my thoughts."

"Dangerous thing, thinking."

He smiled. "Yes. Potentially. Good thing it is a rare event for most of us."

She nodded as she smiled and lifted her coffee cup towards him and descended into her paper again.

Romeo noticed her as though for the first time, taking in her relaxed body angled on the hard shabby chic bench that they both shared, albeit on different tables. She had money. That was clear. Her clothing was very expensively trying to look not expensive. She was eating in a very earthy café that served all the fashionable food without looking fashionable. It was why he enjoyed it there. The food was expensive enough to make the café profitable and keep out the builders and rougher crowd. It was full of pseudo hipsters, mothers who did yoga and Pilates and families with young children who didn't mind spending £50, collectively, on breakfast.

He lowered his chin and began to scribble but his mind was on the curve of her shoulder and the slight upturn of the corner of her mouth. She wore an interesting pendant but he couldn't make out the details. She finished and left, turning just the slightest towards him to nod as she did so. Her coffee cup remained, along with her copy of the Guardian and Times papers. He tried to remember the line that she created with her legs.

It was by pure chance that he met up with her later that day. Her name, he discovered, was Susan.

The Derainier Estate, Sussex
May 2019

Susan's cab arrived shortly after six. The effects of the afternoon was wearing off. She made her way to her room as if just waking from a dream, not knowing how or if she paid the fare.

Sitting on her bed, she looked at her legs as they pointed and flexed her calves. She stood, finding the full length mirror and turned sideways to apprise herself of herself. Her hand touched her belly lightly, feeling a softness that covered the hard core muscles beneath. She lifted her dress, and stood in her bra and underwear, turning to see how much was hanging in and how much hanging out. She was generally pleased with what she saw and she ran her hands through her hair, letting if fall open over her shoulders and down her back.

"Not bad," a male voice said.

She startled, and reached for something to cover herself. She was too far from the bed where her clothes were lying. She covered her chest with her right arm, and protected her lower area with her left. It was pointless, but down without thought.

"Don't let me stop you," the same voice said.

"Robert," she said evenly, forcing herself to remain calm. "This is inappropriate."

"Your door was open. I thought Paul was here." He leaned against the frame of the door, not moving.

"He isn't here."

"How was your day." His eyes locked on hers.

"Fine, thank you." She moved backwards towards the bed. "Can you please let me get dressed?" She felt a stillness in the air.

"I thought you left the door open for a reason." He took a step inside.

"Robert. Please."

"You look amazing."

"Don't."

"Do you know how beautiful you are?"

Susan's right hand flicked up to her neck, then back over her chest. "What are you doing? You can't be in here."

Robert stalked the ten steps from the door to the bed. He stood in front of Susan, never taking his eyes off hers.

"I've seen you look at me over the years."

"Robert, please. You're scaring me."

"I've never done anything about it because you're with Paul. And I, well, I've been all over the place."

He put his hand gently to her face and brushed a lock of hair that had fallen forward. Susan stood rigid in place, hands by her sides. Standing for three, perhaps four, seconds like this, Bob's face softened as he watched two tears exit Susan's left eye. Another part in him hardened and he stepped back. He watched the tears roll down her cheek and settle on her jawline before falling gently onto her chest. His eyes followed the tear as it disappeared into her bra.

It was at this precise moment when her body jerked violently.

Bob's eyes flashed darkness and light as the pain registered. He fell to his knees, then floor, as he clutched his testicles. Susan delivered the next kick into his face and his eyes closed. Able to move again, she grabbed the clothes from the bed behind her blindly and raced to her bedroom door. Down the stairs, through the lounge, into the kitchen where the keys sat on the counter nearest the door. She grabbed them without looking and hit the door running.

The Vogue sat in the drive and she reached for the door. It opened willingly in response to the key's presence. She slammed it and pressed the lock button. Hands shaking, she pushed the start button. Nothing happened. She put her foot on the brake and pushed the button again. Nothing. Panic rose as she looked over her shoulder. Her clothes were still clutched in her right hand and she threw them on the passenger seat. She looked at the key. It was the right one. It must be, she thought; the door opened. She threw it in the centre console area and gripped the wheel. Her heart beat pounded in her ears. Sweat stung her eyes. Her bare feet felt the horizontal rubber on the brake. Her left hand pushed the start button again and the radio came alive, bursting with a Whitney Huston ballad. Her hand retracted and she looked, as if for the first time, what she was pushing. A half-laugh lifted her chest as she found the correct start button and pushed it. The car's V-8 engine came to life with a confident power that was muffled by the internal rubber seals and leather comforts. Susan watched the dashboard come to life. Her left hand reflexively slid to the dial that rose and she turned it, putting the car into drive.

Her body shook as she took one last look over her shoulder and drove as calmly as she could. The tyres spun and the pebbles sprayed backwards. The car lunged forward and she took her foot off the pedal briefly. Then back on. She had lost the finer sense of touch in her foot. It felt like her right foot was a block of wood. As if it was asleep. Attached to her but not in control by her. The car pulled itself and its occupant around the house and into the woods. The mile-long drive. The countless deer and rabbits and invisible residents eyed her silently. Indifferently. They knew the sound of that beast. It was not a threat.

Susan's teeth began to clatter. Her shoulders turned in and the shaking became uncontrollable. She drove on, unwilling to stop while still on the estate. Just a bit further. She could put on her clothes, get something to eat, and assess what the hell just happened once she was out of there. The curve of the road forced her to slow down. It was a blind corner that was designed originally to impress visitors as the landscaped estate unfolded itself before them. Today, Susan swore at every feature, every hole, and even every tree that slowed her escape. The drive was only wide enough for one car to pass. Special passing lanes were incorporated to allow polite exchanges of traffic but it was never designed for more than the Master, his servants, and guests to use. Other tracks existed for farm machinery and the help to move around. As she rounded the curve, her foot rested gently on the brake out of practice. Anything could be coming as she slowed the car to a medium running pace as it navigated the curve.

Her eye extended along the road, willing it to show itself and allow her to accelerate to safety. Rhododendrons, cedars, oaks, and lime trees blurred into a green and earthy brown; an indistinct background as her vision tunnelled. Her foot stamped on the brake before her brain could register it. Her body strained against the taught seatbelt and the car came to a halt.

In front of her, occupying most of the drive, was a magnificent buck. Its antlers spanned the length of a lying man. Its head was turned to look directly at the oncoming intruder, something oozing from one its nostrils. Susan stared back, unable to process the wild animal unafraid.

Two smaller bucks emerged and bolted across, their antlers little more than pricks on their crown. A burst of bodies followed, all does, each frenetic in their fear of the metal beast. The alpha buck stood still, lowering its antlers at the car's grill. Susan's heart slowed at the wonder of the scene before her, momentarily forgetting her fear of the scene behind her.

The massive buck raised its head, took in the safety of its charge, and disappeared into the woods.

Her foot tentatively lifted off the brake, and the car rolled effortlessly forward. The drive straightened and she could see the chimney of the lodge house that sat on the entrance to the estate. Her foot moved to the accelerator and pushed down. The car pulled itself forward, fast.

Susan gripped the steering wheel. The automatic windshield wipers were activated by a flurry of seeds. The sudden movement caused her to jerk the wheel but she regained control.

There was no stop sign at the end of the drive where it met the highway. The green hedges of the lodge were tall and were cut next to the road. Her visibility splay was pathetic. She always complained of this to Paul in the past. Ignoring caution, she pushed her foot down and accelerated into the coming darkness.

Two hours later, there was a knock at her hotel room.

"I came as soon as I could." Candace dropped clinking bags on the floor and put her arms around her friend.

"You're a star, sweetheart." Susan was in a white robe, free from any insignia or logo. She shuffled in and Candace followed, bags betraying their contents on pickup and drop-off.

"Have you spoken to him?"

"I've been ringing every number and every person. Nothing."

"Odd."

"And then some."

"You thinking what I'm thinking?"

"Yeah. The asshole."

"Drink?"

"Already there."

"I'll join you."

"What a disaster."

"What are you going to do?"

"I'm not sure."

"Are you going back?"

"I haven't thought that far."

"What about, you know, him?"

"The brother?" Susan's hand went to her neck.

"Yeah."

"I can't see being anywhere that he is."

"For Christ's sake, I was thinking about more than that."

"Criminal charges?"

"Or hitman. I know a few muscle heads that can help you out with that."

"I just want to talk to Paul."

"Have you called the one person you haven't?"

"I don't have her number."

"Are you sure?"

Susan shot Candace a look that said not to go any further, at least not now.

"I've left dozens of messages. He will call me when he turns on his phones."

"When is the last time you've turned off your phone? Or had your battery go dead for that matter?"

"Never. I don't know why they use that excuse. It is so predictable."

"So pathetic."

"So childish." Susan grabbed her hair and twisted it into a knot then let it fall. She rubbed her chest where the robe opened. "You know; they want to be men. To be 'the man'. To be in control. Such a load of crap. At least man up and admit to it."

On cue, her phone rang. Both women stared at it. Chimes mixed with a rumbling vibration of phone on laminate alerted them someone wanted to talk. Susan picked up the phone off the side table and saw the name. She mouthed 'Paul' to Candace and pressed the green button.

"Where the hell have you been?"

"In the gym. I just saw your missed calls." The voice was strained. Trying too hard, Susan thought.

"Let me tell you something," she interrupted.

Paul continued but she was not prepared to listen.

"No. Let me tell you something," Susan repeated. "I'm not even angry about what you get up to. No, don't interrupt. I'm not even angry. Disappointed, yes. But that is for another day. Have you talked to that ass-hole brother of yours?"

Silence for a full two seconds. Then, "Yeah."

"What did he say?" Susan was quiet and moved the phone from her right to left ear, opening and closing her right hand in Candace's direction. A drink was duly placed in the now-content hand.

"Something about an argument. He made it out as though it was nothing."

"And you believe him?"

"He was bleeding. Said you sucker-punched him." Again, the same strained voice.

"I barely touched him. Are you listening to yourself?"

"He's pretty shaken up over everything."

"That's ridiculous."

"Don't you think you should come home and we'll talk this all through like adults?"

"And that's your position?" Red splotches crept up her neck as she finished the contents of her glass.

"I don't think that you are acting reasonably…"

"Paul, what the—"

"Let me know where you are, Susan, and I'll pick you up. Everything will be fine."

"I'm not going to tell you where I am. I am not feeling particularly safe. Thanks to your fucking brother."

Silence on the other end.

"Paul, let me say this. I am this close to screaming uncontrollably and checking into the Priory. You aren't standing up for me. At all. If I keep talking, I'm going to say something I'm going to regret. No. Please. I'm going to hang up. Don't call me."

Susan slowly lowered her arm to her lap, turned the phone screen towards herself and held the button that turned off her phone. Calmly, she placed it next to her bed. Candace silently watched, a horror crossing her face as she witnessed a new pain on her best friend's face.

Susan pushed herself against the headboard and pulled two pillows next to her, clutching them tightly. Her face appeared calm despite the tendons in her neck standing out. Her chest rose and fell. Her drink was gone. Candace refilled it, then cuddled next to her.

The two sat in silence, allowing the other to hold their hand. Tears began to fall down Candace's cheek. Susan reached over tenderly and wiped them away.

"I'll be fine, my love. Everything will be fine."

"But this isn't how it's supposed to be," Candace cried. "What the fuck! What the fuck fuck fuck!!! You can stay calm as Buddha and Sid, but I won't sit by and let this shit happen. We've got to do something."

"Tonight we sit and be," Susan said. "There will be time enough for tears later."

She stared straight ahead at the bland patterns on the hotel wall. She felt Candace place her head on her shoulder. She thought she could even feel the tears but dismissed that as impossible through the robe.

"Screw 'em."

Candace, startled, sat up. "Huh?"

"Screw 'em all." Susan repeated.

"Exactly, let's fuck them bastards up. What's the plan?"

"I know someone with a plan."

Candace took a moment to think. "Don't tell me you're going to ask a man to help?" Her voice was disappointed.

"Not a man. A person. Romeo."

"Loverboy, more like it." Candace never disapproved of a little fun.

"You'll see what I mean."

Susan got up and threw off her robe. Her body was strong, flush with the heat of the robe.

"We're going somewhere?"

"Yes."

"No time like the present kind of thing?"

"Yep."

"Late night bootie call?"

"No."

"Are you going to tell me what we're doing?"

"On the way." She was already half dressed.

"Are we driving or being driven?"

Susan paused briefly and looked at Candace, exaggerated a weaving motion, and returned to getting dressed.

"Driven it is," Candace said.

Hampstead, London (May 2019)

A string broke when Susan took that call from Paul. You never know which string is holding you up until it snaps. We are all marionettes; more than Pinocchio, but far from a god.

Susan's driver stopped in front of Romeo's. He was expecting her and the door opened as soon as the taxi stopped. She walked, head erect, up the landscaped walkway, barely noticing the freshly cut grass or the occasional clump of compost that a sloppy gardener had left on the path. Candace had wisely allowed herself to be dropped off at her own home first.

"You said it was urgent," Romeo said as she brushed gently past him. Intentionally.

She left her stilettos on, the sound creating a distinctive snap of pressure and wood composite against the oiled wood floors. Romeo followed her in, noticing an anger in her step that he was unfamiliar with.

The tone changed as she moved from hardwood to marble tile. The sound stopped as she found the fridge, initially confusing due to it being integrated into the kitchen woodwork. She glanced at Romeo as she put her hand on the fridge door, as if waiting for permission. Romeo caught on and shrugged slightly while his left hand rotated, as if to say, "go ahead."

There was a clink of glass on glass and a bottle of white wine came out, was opened and poured into glasses that he had quickly put in place. He was waiting for her to speak.

Instead, she turned and put herself next to him, tracing the collar of his open shirt.

"I need to be with you," she said softly.

"I want you to be with me, too. What's happened?"

"Can't you kiss a girl and just shut up? Turn off that brain, close your eyes, and…"

He leaned in and kissed her gently, causing her to stop. She put her hand to his face and closed her eyes. He tasted wonderful, she thought.

"What happened?" Romeo repeated, pulling back slightly, arms still around her.

"My husband's an asshole."

Romeo stayed silent. Waiting.

"I thought you wanted me," she pouted, pushing at his chest. Her body was a swirl of emotions. Part of her wanted to claw at his clothes, make him take her on the table or floor, and blot out the ceaseless noise of her life's mistakes.

"I thought you believed in love," he replied. A corner of his mouth lifted. His hands were reaching tentatively towards her. They touched her hands. She linked her little finger over his, then slid it over his hand and pulled him towards her.

"I do."

"Which is why you will stay in my spare room. I'll stay in mine."

Susan dropped her hands and flushed. "Are you kidding me? I throw myself at you and you put me in the doghouse? Have I become that woman? So insecure, needy?" She put her head down.

"You are not needy or insecure. An insecure woman wouldn't do what you just did. You want something and you are taking it. If I didn't feel something real for you, I'd be all over you right now. But the sun will rise again and I want to spend the rest of my life watching the sun rise with you. Not just once."

She lifted her head.

"My body is shaking, it wants you so much right now," he continued. "But you don't find people like you very often in life. I may regret this. I am regretting it already."

Susan put her lips on his and held his hair to keep him from moving. When she broke for air, his eyes were shut and his arms were tracing her body. She kissed him with a passion she hadn't felt since Marcel. She felt for the buttons on his shirt and began fiddling with them, then pulled his shirt off. He let her.

She traced his body with the tip of her finger, occasionally leaning in to kiss, smiling and kissing Romeo in between. All thought of sleeping in separate rooms was forgotten. The two entwined their bodies, releasing a lifetime of longing for something they didn't know they wanted.

The next morning, warm from each other's body and the goose down duvet, Susan felt no guilt. A smile sat on her face as she glimpsed at Romeo and took in the room. It was large, masculine and stark. The emperor sized bed sat between two large oak side tables topped with marble. The walls were covered in panelling and shelves with doors that led to a walk-in wardrobe, bathroom and separate toilet. Three large windows overlooked the garden and the brick wall that surrounded it. A massive seventy-two-inch television was set flush into the wall with a panel that discretely covered it when not wanted. There was a mannequin in the corner complete with a suit, shirt and shoes next to it. Their clothes were strewn over the silk carpet which covered the entire floor area. Its Arabic patterns the only explosive colour apart from greenery of the trees outside. There was not one photo on the walls or on the side tables.

Her mind wanted to simply take it all in. *To be*, as the new-agers said. But, could a sentient being merely exist? To simply 'be'? Great yogi-speak, she thought, as she cuddled next to her new lover. Transcending to a place that disengaged the mind while being impractical for real people day in day out. Her hands wrapped his body next to hers. Fine for the very rich and very poor, she thought. Her mind kept following the train of thought while her body fought for a repeat of last night. Romeo's body responded and she put her philosophising on hold.

In the shower, body getting hungry, Susan felt that there was a philosophy for the burdened class, formerly known as the middle class, that needed articulating. How could she, privileged that she was, be that person? Was Romeo mad or inspired? *In all things, balance,* she responded. A balance on engagement with one's environment along with disengagement (ie. to 'be') was key. Sleep was critical but one mustn't (nor could one) sleep all day. How did this relate to Romeo's bloody screws? What insanity. A real solution was a work in progress, individually tailored. It required effort by the individual as it necessitated a very difficult procedure: to know oneself.

The sound of the shower faded as she went through the maze that bridged the love that she felt last night with the person who was contemplating the systematic sabotage of a culture and country's infrastructure.

Her coffee was perfect. Her body warm and cosy in the robes Romeo retrieved from heated radiators. They sat outside in silence, looking out onto the piece of London they were able to share from the bedroom balcony. Her hand dropped next to his and linked her little finger into his. It caused her to smile and all internal arguments faded. She had found a soul with whom she could happily spend her remaining years.

Chapter 9

Eight Months Later…Hampstead, London (2020)

"What happens when you finally find happiness?" Susan rolled to her side, next to Romeo, and stared at the ceiling with its intricate cornicing.

"Stay happy, I guess."

"Are you happy?" Her voice betrayed an insecurity she didn't feel.

Romeo put his arms around her and pulled her closer. The morning stubble of his otherwise freshly shaved face tickled her in a nice way. "Incredibly so," he said, then kissed her gently.

"It's just so good," her voice trailed off.

"These last few months have passed in a blink. I fear the rest of our lives will too. Why not spend that blink being happy?" Romeo's hand traced her body as he spoke.

Susan squirmed backwards with a smile and sat up, back against the headboard.

"Can I ask you something?" she said while trying unsuccessfully to suppress a smile.

"Sure." Romeo stayed lying down, looking up at her.

"I'm serious," she said.

"So am I."

Susan took his hand. "This moment is perfect."

Romeo kissed her knees and thigh in response.

"You love me," she continued.

He kissed he area around her belly button.

"Will you marry me?" The words flew out of her mouth as if by surprise. She knew that the one place you should never propose is in bed. And she just did it. Her body tensed.

Romeo stopped kissing and looked up at her. His hand was tracing her body and he pulled himself level with her. He was silent as he caressed her face and looked deeply into her eyes, looking for something even he was uncertain of.

Susan began to shake but waited for his reply.

"Yes, my love. Yes, a million times, yes."

He kissed her and she tasted his tears.

Neither of them broached the uncomfortable and inconvenient truth that she was still married.

Chapter 10

PART TWO—Brothers Twenty-Three Years Earlier…Winter, 1997, Winnipeg, Canada

A greasy spoon. Two desperate brothers. Youth, and ambition. February, 1997, Canada. Paul, and his brother Robert, from a small town no-one had ever heard of nor cared enough to even ask of, sat in huddled discussion at the table nearest the toilet but also the furthest from anyone in Salisbury House, a cafe frequented by students, police, and a certain generation nostalgic of the 50's and 60's. Two in the morning and the coffee was still strong enough to melt a spoon. The Winnipeg weather had covered the windows at first with cute winter wonderland crystals but now were icing over. This, despite being triple glazed. The February cold was made colder from an Arctic blast that carried with it a twenty degree drop in normal temperatures. Schools were closed, employees found excuses to miss work, and cars that weren't plugged in overnight refused to start in the morning. The only place that seemed indifferent to the cold was the iconic greasy spoon that welcomed RCMPs, bikers, travelling salespeople, families and the two brothers with equanimity.

"We have enough. Let's just call it quits and live our lives. Face it, would you have expected to have nearly a million bucks?" Paul sat back against his seat in satisfaction.

"It's a good start. Now we can play with the bigger boys. We'll turn that into ten or even a hundred. They don't have our hunger. They don't know where we've been or what we've had to face. They're all soft. We'll eat them alive." Robert's eyes shone.

Paul inhaled deeply through his nose and sat back. His Canada Goose anti-exposure jacket hugged him as he sat back. He leaned forward and pushed it aside. His hands played with the creamers in their plastic cups. He used to drink those creamers with his father in this same shop.

"I don't know, Rob. It's a lot of money. It's real. It's in the bank. No bullshit. No dreams. We cut it in half and go our ways. Buy an apartment block or three and live off the rents. No problem."

"Pff. You and you small dreams. Don't you want to be like Mr. Bergen with 4,000 apartments? Or those families in Toronto with 40,000 apartments? You can't do that with a measly million."

"True. But we can live comfortably the rest of our lives on the income that our capital can produce."

"What are you? A book? Where're your balls? We've got capital. Real money. Blood. With our guts and that money, we can eventually be bigger than Leo. We can be billionaires."

The word resonated in Paul's head. It was true. Being a millionaire wasn't what it once was. Anyone could become a millionaire. Hell, he and his brother just did it. His tongue rubbed back and forth against his bottom teeth. Then, sucked invisible bits from between his teeth.

"What would you do?" As he said the words, he knew Rob had him. He saw the edge of Rob's mouth turn up in partial triumph.

"Leave it to me. I'll make us a hundred times this in the next few years."

"Legally?"

"More or less."

"What happens if we get caught?"

"That's the beauty. 'We' can't get caught. Only I can. You'll be long gone."

"Wha-?"

"If we do this right, I want to copy what successful people do. They create a safe pair of hands and siphon off money just in case things go wrong."

"That's fraud. Money laundering."

"No. We'll structure it. You are my brother. We can't change that. But we can create some distance. These things always go wrong due to a betrayal of sorts. We need to trust each other completely."

Paul looked at his brother. Robert's eyes glistened unnaturally and his face basked in the glow. He believed whatever he was saying.

"I'm not sure I like what I am about to hear."

"It's nothing. I'm not talking about running drugs or doing anything like that. But if you want to make this work, you need to have plausible deniability."

"We don't have that much, you know. Just a million. And that was bloody hard to get, don't forget. What if you lose it all?"

"I won't."

"What if you do?"

"I promise to kill myself."

A trickle of electricity poured from the back of Paul's tongue to the centre of his gut. His muscles felt a jolt of adrenaline and his head twitched.

"Don't talk shit."

"I will kill everyone before I let them take our money." He wasn't smiling and his eyes bore into Paul's.

"Have some water or coffee. Maybe a beer?"

"I'm fine. I want you to know that I'm serious."

"Maybe you need to lighten up?"

"Look. You got us here. And I'm grateful. But I can get us to the next level. You know that. I know that. All you need to do is step aside, be the safe pair of hands, and let me rock and roll." He sat back and lifted his coffee to his lips. It was cool and he finished the cup.

"Maybe we continue what we're doing? We are okay."

"Are Mom and Dad okay? Are any of us okay? Really? We can spend a million and not even touch the sides for the needs of everyone. I say we focus and go for it."

"Mom and Dad raised a family. They couldn't take chances. They paid their bills and gave us an education."

"We're not talking about them. We are not them. We are us. Just us. No family, no money, no friends. Just two brothers crazy enough to chase a dream. To have more. To be more."

"Sounds like an army recruitment ad."

"Be all you can be, baby." Robert was grinning. "We can smash this and change our lives and everyone around us."

Paul heard the words. Those were the words that woke him at 4.30 every morning and kept him going until 11 o'clock at night. He was still small fry. He knew that. But he was a long way from 99% of the rest of the country who had a few months' savings and worked like dogs every day. At least his dog day was his choosing.

"How would it work?"

"Like Cy said, any tax or corporate structure needs a safe pair of hands. There can be no notes, no links, no nothing. You trust me and I trust you. You take, say, fifty grand and fuck off to the States or Europe and live your life."

"Fifty kay? And do what? Flip burgers while you burn through our capital?"

"You have to trust me, Paul."

Both lips were sucked into Paul's mouth as his teeth bit down. Robert was his older brother. He was the dynamo behind all their ventures. But, so far, he always ended up with nothing. Why would this time be different? He wanted to say this but something kept him quiet. The quiet confidence that Robert held in Paul. The girls he introduced him to. The whore house that he pulled him out of on a particularly bad weekend of self-loathing. Images of the asshole he threw down a flight of stairs. 'Peter Pan', Robert laughed when Paul recounted the situation. The addict had been nagging and poking Paul and he did it one too many times. Without warning, Paul picked him up and tossed him down the stairs. The body flew like garbage in a sack, hitting the stairs two thirds down and tumbling into a pile. Not content, Paul stomped downstairs and dragged the inert body outside into minus 25-degree weather. He would have left him there. He didn't know if he was dead or not. Robert didn't blame him. Didn't ask anything. He checked the pulse. Covered him with a blanket and called the ambulance. The druggee had no voice in the matter. No one listened to his version of events. The matter was forgotten apart from the words 'Peter Pan' with a chuckle from Robert after they were well into their cups.

"I don't like it," Paul said eventually.

"What's not to like? Go to India. Get laid on every continent. Get drunk, unwind. Forget about the world that you carry on your shoulders for a bit. It won't go away. I'll sort out the rest."

The idea was appealing. He didn't need much to live on. Two grand a month was more than enough to travel cockroach class. "And how am I supposed to be your safe pair of hands? Just for argument's sake."

"I'll pay you either dividends or royalties or a licence. You take the money and make it disappear. That, I know you can do. Bounce it around a bit. Different jurisdictions, different companies. Find a way to buy an asset clean from any connection to the past. I'll feed you whatever I can."

Robert reached across the table and pushed aside the thick porcelain coffee mugs full of cooling coffee and grabbed Paul's hands. He had never done this before and it startled Paul.

"I'll never let you down. If I burn in hell or kill a hundred people, I'll make you more money than you could have hoped for. Let me stain my soul. Go and live your life. You have always been the Joseph of the family. Do something good with your life. I'll worry about the money."

Paul felt his throat close and tears well. His hands shook slightly as adrenaline coursed through his body. He wanted to be the good guy. But he wanted the money and power even more. The tension made his biceps hurt. He nodded and they planned a future.

***

He knew, and he didn't. He heard whispers of a tax carousel, where tax (usually VAT/GST) was "disappeared" from a series of transactions. The government called this tax fraud. It could be extremely profitable for those running it—especially if they had a fall guy neatly in place. Paul figured that Robert found these fall guys and paid them enough to do the time if caught. For Paul, he received his daily and weekly payments. He did his part. He "disappeared" those funds. Made them safe.

And this was only one branch of Robert's ever-growing money tree.

Paul marvelled at the power of an idea. Decided upon by a handful of people seated in boardrooms or a humble coffee shop. Acted upon with the aid of capital. Impacting everyone and everything.

"Turn on the television!" Paul could hear her voice shaking from intensity.

"I'm in town. Just going into a meeting. What's going on?" His voice was curt. She was beginning to annoy him. A couple of dates and she thought she was his girlfriend. He would need to contact the agency and get another secretary.

"Any station. Paul?"

He pressed the red button on his Nokia. When he got his first mobile, he loved everything about it. Now, it was starting to annoy him. He would watch the evening news when he got home after drinks with the boys.

His hand went seamlessly into his jacket inside pocket and deposited the phone. Canali; he liked the Italian suits. Shoes, Church's. The English design fit him best. Ties varied, but mainly Italian. His ex was Italian. Nothing like the temp. Passionate, slightly crazy, and smarter than anyone he had ever met before. The perfect life partner. Until his brother messed things up.

He put the thought out of his head and pushed his way through the crowds as he emerged from the underground. He was a few minutes early. He enjoyed strolling the streets before important meetings. The glass monuments, ever larger and technically sophisticated, beckoned his ambition. The heavy glass doors. The security clearance and name badge as he entered. The understanding as he announced who he was meeting. The attractive girl or guy who stood when he arrived. The proffered coffee or "anything else" with a smile as he was ushered into a waiting area. Always with heavy armchairs, sometimes traditional, this time modern. Always with a massive flat screen television on the wall with the sound off. Always tuned to BBC. Two copies of the Telegraph, Times, and FT sat neatly in anticipation on the glass table that inevitably filled the space between armchairs and wall.

He unbuttoned his jacket and sat down. He picked up the FT and sat back, scanning the headlines. The television caught his eye and he watched, not sure what he was seeing. It was not yet three and there was a picture of one of the World Trade Towers billowing smoke. He put the paper down and looked closer.

"Can we turn on the sound?" He asked to no-one in particular. He scanned the surrounding for a remote but couldn't find anything. He stood up and walked closer to the screen.

A young man, impeccably dressed and cleanly shaven, appeared and stopped as he saw what was on the television.

"Holy shit," he said to himself. Then, "Sorry", as he registered Paul's presence. He pushed a panel and pivoted the television towards him. He pushed a button and the sound emerged.

Paul's ears felt muffled by the change of atmosphere.

More staff appeared and, soon, fifteen people stood watching.

"Oh my God," a woman said softly. An object flew into the second tower. The CNN announcer stuttered briefly before returning to the same narrative.

Paul felt a tingle of cold from his head to his sternum radiate and repeat three times. It was as though his soul shuddered.

No one spoke for a moment as they took in what they were seeing. It was virtually unthinkable. Flight 175 crashed into the second World Trade Centre building at 590 miles per hour. Both towers were smoking. This was probably war. A lot of people were dying in front of their eyes. They were reassured that, at least, the towers would stand and all survivors should be able to get out.

Paul sat down and dialled Robert. "You seeing this?" He was too exhausted to say more.

"Yeah." The voice was also empty.

"Holy shit, eh?"

"Yeah. You OK?"

"I'm okay. In London. About to go into a meeting. You?"

"I'm in Toronto. Just taking the week off. I'm gonna call Ma and Pa. Talk to you later."

And he was gone. Paul felt better. He'd talk to his parents after his meeting. He sat back and watched everyone in the room. Every person was on their phone. The crowd had doubled. There was no more space. He heard "I love you" from every conversation. It made him feel lonelier than he ever felt before. He had no one to tell "I love you" to.

***

Business came naturally to Paul. He wanted to be an artist, maybe a musician or writer. But making money was what seemed to come easily. He could see angles that others either ignored or couldn't see. It took a while for him to realise that this was a gift. There may have been sharper minds within the various systems of shares and stock or company management; but there was no better mind than his to survive as an individual under the radar and amass an independence that would provide for him to live a hundred lifetimes.

Years passed, and Paul continued to do what he did best. Accumulate, disappear funds, and speculate. He invested his money evenly between property and stocks. In property, he chose commercial and residential in Mayfair and Kensington. In stocks, he chose tracker funds for each of three continents—North America, Europe and Asia. His objective was capital preservation. If he made money, even better.

His personal home was in the country, away from the noise and pollution of the big city. A former hunting ground of King Henry VIII. Established gardens, ancient woodlands, and a home set in enough land to keep any nosey person far enough away.

The mantra remained simple. Don't ask, don't tell. When Robert visited, he never stayed at Paul's home. Instead, he took up residence in the Savoy.

Robert's hand shook the doorman's and Paul could see the studied care as the employee received the £50 tip. Doors were opened, of course, but more was done for Robert and Paul than was expected. Their car, a Bentley, was parked outside the door for easy access. Whispers in ears ensured that all of the hotel's staff understood that these were VIPs who knew how to show their appreciation. There was a strict policy of no hookers in the hotel, but Robert seemed to find a very willing supply of very attractive dates. No questions were raised by the staff.

By 2013, Icarus flew too close to the sun and his wings melted. Robert was arrested on a trumped up charge by a disgruntled bookkeeper. She was in love with him and he spurned her advances. She followed him to one of his parties and retrieved a used condom—how, he still couldn't figure out—and used that to claim that he raped her. The evidence was eventually thrown out but he was on the radar of the police. When the company backers lost confidence in Robert and pulled out, the whole enterprise unravelled and he was charged with insider trading and sentenced to ten years in prison, eligible for parole in five. He entered Otisville prison in 2014 and was released in 2019. Two weeks after getting permission to leave the country from his parole officer, he flew to meet up with Paul.

Chapter 11

Sussex, UK (May 2019)

"I can't hate my brother, even if I hate everything he has done these last twenty or so years." Paul lowered his morning coffee and looked at Susan.

"You can't ask him to come." Susan lowered her morning hot chocolate and looked back, locking eyes.

"I have no choice."

"He'll be arrested. Worse, you may be arrested."

"I have to take that chance."

"Even if it kills you."

"It won't come to that." *At least, I hope not*, Paul thought to himself.

Susan put down her cup a little too abruptly and some of the dark chocolate spilt onto the kitchen table. "We don't owe him anything," she said.

Paul was lost in thought. "Maybe. But I feel as though I still do."

He looked out over the undulations beyond his sculptured garden that could have been painted by Constable. A two-hundred-year-old Lebanese Cyprus tree spread its boughs gracefully half way to a shallow pond that attracted Canadian geese and local mallards as well as a persistent heron that kept the fish population in check. Two magnificent Redwood trees towered over the landscape marred only by the tops that broke off in the storm of 1987. Colorful rhododendrons from Tibet were growing happily like weeds throughout his thousand-acre estate.

"I already called him." Paul looked at Susan as he said it. His insides twitched as he braced for the blast. There was always a tension when they talked about his family.

Her lips straightened into a line and three more lines appeared on her forehead but she said nothing. She leaned back and took another sip.

"He's arriving tomorrow," Paul continued. His shoulders felt the tension. The cords in his neck tightened and he made a mental note to see Zara before Robert arrived. "I'll pick him up."

Susan nodded and got up to leave. "Do you need me for anything?" She touched the pendant on the necklace that hung over her turtleneck sweater.

"Do you feel like making a roast?" As he said the words, his stomach puckered. A shudder of spasm shook his insides, behind his sternum.

There was a slight pause, mid-way as she stood, before she straightened up tall. "I'll get Gloria to put something together. I forgot about an appointment I have in London. I don't think I'll be back until late." There was a gentle clink as her china cup settled into its saucer followed by a determined staccato of her heels against the marbled floor as she left the room.

Paul relaxed into his chair and pulled out a cigar. His body thumped with a pulse that he felt in his forearms. He strained to hear Susan's voice or footsteps. His breathing increased as he willed himself to locate her sounds. Nothing. He had to go outside to enjoy the cigar but it was still a pleasure to smell and hold before the actual act of smoking took place. It was one of the few vices he allowed himself as it forced him to sit still for almost an hour. He opened a door high up above the Aga and pulled out a bottle of 25-year-old Laphroaig single malt whiskey and made his way outside to sit under the cedar. He made a note about the early hour, then disregarded it. What was the point of having money and still be a slave to time?

The weather was pleasant. Paul wore his grandfather's old leather jacket. The smell of cigars and pipes always reminded Paul of his childhood. Far away from the intrigue he and Robert had created. Back in a time where a little boy could spend time with his grandfather with nothing to do other than watch the day pass.

And, in that time warp, the smell was not of fresh grass or the breeze that rustled the laundry hanging in the garden. It was the quiet enjoyment of a cigar. Paul tried to cut them out and someday would. But there was nothing like a morning cigar. He would brush and floss and gargle before he went to Zara. Maybe even change.

Two mallards, one colorful male and the brown female, swam to the far side of the pond when he sat down. The bench was a souvenir from a trip to India a decade ago. Overly ornate but he had grown to love it. The wrought iron and teak wood held his weight effortlessly. The longer he waited, the more he wanted to see Zara. The cigar had already been cut, and he had been sucking on it since he was still in the house. His lips and tongue had reached their fill of the rich tannins on the tobacco leaf. His teeth were discoloured despite best efforts from his dentist to clean them. Between coffee and the cigar, he knew that he became an intolerable stench if it wasn't for the whiskey. He preferred it cask strength, making it over 55% alcohol by volume. A man's drink.

He lit the cigar and sat back, crossing his outstretched legs at the ankles. Soon the ducks would return, hoping for some bread which he forgot this time. Even the geese would begin their strut around the pond. The goslings would stay behind with the mother as the father established his territory. Despite some initial hissing, the father goose was prepared to accept food almost from Paul's hand. He still needed to toss it about a meter from him which was close enough. It was just a matter of time before the goslings followed suit.

Paul closed his eyes to a red black white mist of indistinguishable soundless noise. Shapes that he was looking at faded from within a darkness visible to a uniformity without pattern. In the past, he would have searched for signs or messages. Today, he sat and enjoyed the unknowable. His leaden glass was a little heavier with the caramel whiskey, no ice. He felt the world slip away, occasionally hearing a bird's wings and the nestling of trees too close to each other. Emptiness was his objective and he allowed himself to swing his legs across and lie down on the Indian bench. The whiskey's cork slid in and out with barely a squeaky pop as he refilled his glass. The iron was less harsh against the side of his head. Half of the bottle disappeared as Paul's breathing reverted to a sleep pattern and he could attempt nothing nor control anything until his body was ready.

Three fallow deer startled when his body moved again. A large inhalation and slow movement of legs and torso as he righted himself. The sun had crossed the horizon, still warm with a hint of the evening to come. Paul wiped drool from his collar and rotated his head. It was time to see Zara. He texted her, gathered his bottle, and brushed ash from his jacket. If he timed things right, he could still grab some leftovers, coffee, have a shower, and brush his teeth. No woman liked a man who stank.

***

But there was only one life. And Susan was his choice of wife. She was perfect. Smart, beautiful, and wise. There were mysteries that she kept close to herself, but he didn't need or want to know about them. This was part of the attraction they had for each other.

Then why was he seeing Zara? He was rich, healthy, married to a woman whom he loved and who loved him. As he drove home in his Range Rover Vogue, he pictured his first vehicle—a VW banger—and the distance, both geographically and mentally, from his childhood to his present. His family was one of fringe characters.

It was this irrational fear and his desire to be more mainstream that drove him to have an affair. He wanted to be normal. To be like everyone else.

In the process, he risked destroying the serenity and sanctity of his marriage and the trust of a good woman. At the same time, the thrill of the danger excited him even more. It gave him an insight into the weakness of men and the temptations that most people succumbed to. He felt superior without any irony.

∞

Sometimes, it was little more than mechanical. Many times, it was good—relaxing and enjoyable; a release from pent up energy. Then, there were the times that defied description. When the warmth of her body imperceptibly caressed his. Their lips kissing, fingers touching, eyes searching each other as time melted away beneath her sheets. The natural motion of two animals orchestrated by an unseen hand. Anxiety, thought, all of the world he knew cerebrally, fell away. Just the moist rhythm and a building pressure. When the moment came, hips flexed inwards, muscles in his knees and torso taught with expectation, the pulsing expulsion of him into her; he ceased to be Paul and became all of mankind. Zara, his Eve. The act, their fruit. His eyes flickered with the body shudder as the last ejaculate made its course. Her body, sheened with exertion from her own moment, glowed with heat. Her arms pulled him towards her, him still inside, to lie on top. A salty kiss as he brushed away matted hair on her. He pulled himself off her slowly to a small gasp when they parted. She rolled on her side and he pulled a light cotton sheet over the two of them as they lay, spooning, not having spoken a word.

Paul closed his eyes to the perfect moment and drifted asleep. Zara had already grabbed his hand and put it to her breast. He instinctively squeezed gently, caressed, then held. His forefinger traced her raised nipple and the dimples that surrounded it. Their bodies breathed as one. The sliding door let in the perfumed air of spring honey blossom and lilacs, gently pushing against the muslin that turned the outside into an indistinct white. A woodpecker's staccato against the Scotch pines was joined by a select chorus of unknown, to Paul's ear, song birds. Not as fulsome as at first light. Just enough to let you know that you were in the country, at peace, with no predators to upset their spring music.

Chapter 12

The Derainier Estate, Sussex (May 2019)

Paul woke next to Susan. Their love making the previous night was different. Passionate and exploring. As though they were making love for the first time. He liked it and wondered whether he was risking too much with Zara.

He padded softly to their en suite and then downstairs where he made a coffee and was hypnotised by the song birds diving in and out of the full birdfeeders. Paul was transfixed at the single-mindedness. At the song bird's indifference to the squirrels. At the co-existence. Feathers from what looked to have been a pigeon lay scattered on the ground beneath. Most likely compliments of the feral cat that adopted their home three years earlier. The ultimate hunter-killer, the cat.

Robert, now just Bob, slept upstairs. He wouldn't be seeing him until after lunch at the earliest.

He heard a sound and turned around. It was Susan.

"Can't sleep?"

"I slept perfectly. Thanks." She kissed him gently.

Paul didn't understand this behaviour. He was convinced that she knew about Zara. She was distant and cold until just the last few days. Why the change?

"Coffee?" He got up and motioned for her to sit. He poured her a cup, black, and sat next to her. Both looked at the mulberry tree.

"Are you going to tell me the secret?" Her voice was flat, unemotional, and noncommittal as to whether she already knew the answer.

Paul felt a flush as a number of possible secrets flooded his mind. Zara, first. Then, an old one. What's her name? The Chinese girl. He wracked his mind to remember what he said so he didn't trip himself up.

"Sorry?" He asked, trying to buy some time.

"Robert. Bob. Whatever he goes by. Why now?"

"He is travelling on business …"

"Mmmm… Unlikely." Her lips pursed and the three familiar lines appeared on her forehead.

"Ok. He's been in some trouble. He needs money. I'm the only one in the family with anything. It was only natural."

"Was it natural for him to spend a hundred grand on a party at the Savoy and forget to invite us? Or the hookers he would inevitably turn up with? Or the way he paws me? Looks at me? Do you even notice?" Her vein in her forehead was enlarged and she rubbed her neck as she stared at him.

"Uh, no. I know that he's a bit boisterous when partying. But we talked about that time he hugged you. It was nothing. Just a bit of nonsense."

Susan didn't touch her coffee. "He had his hand on my ass for a long time. His fingers were moving, searching. I was too shocked to move away. He was holding me too tight. There were all your friends. Everyone was laughing. That whore had her hands all over you. Maybe that's the real reason you don't give a fuck."

She stood up and walked towards the sink at the opposite end of the kitchen. She paused, then turned slightly towards him. He didn't move. He became quiet, bowing his head and saying nothing. After a few more moments, Susan left the room.

Paul didn't see her the rest of the day. He knew that she would go to London or call a friend and have drinks at the club. She would be all right. She always was. Good old dependable Susan.

Bob came down to the smell of lunch. Steaks with fried tomatoes and chips. A gravy was prepared just in case. Bob asked Gloria to make three eggs for him, fried. The two brothers sat down to eat. Neither talked until most of the steak was done, apart from an initial grunt to acknowledge that the quality of the meat was superb and the preparation sublime.

"It's quite a way from Winnipeg, eh?"

Paul nodded.

"Rest of the family been over here?"

Paul nodded again.

"They didn't stay?"

Paul shook his head. This morning started unpredictably and this conversation had the possibility of stirring up skeletons he'd rather leave buried.

"Do you hear much from everyone?"

"Just the odd call. Now with WhatsApp, we share pictures and chat more often with video." It was true. He refused to use the app for the longest time, calling it the terrorist app because of the encryption technology and that many terrorists were known for using it as a means of communication. Eventually he succumbed due to ease and the fact everyone else was on it.

"Do you know how many times they visited me these last five years?"

Paul remained silent, his jaw clenching, lips pulled in.

"I didn't see you once, by the way."

"You didn't want me to come. That was always part of the plan."

"Yes, the plan. You remember the details?"

"There is no plan."

"That's better. No plan. Just two brothers on opposite sides of the world, working independently. One, taking all the risks. The other, all the rewards."

Paul felt the slow downward electrical current reach his stomach again. His breathing was shallow and increased. He said nothing.

"It's okay to talk here, isn't it? Or are you afraid that there are bugs listening in?"

"This is not a conversation for the breakfast table."

"Then let's go for a walk. You like that, don't you? Walking in your five century's old landscaped surroundings as you mull over how to allocate your capital and who you hope to screw next?"

Paul got up without speaking and nodded to Gloria as she drifted in and cleared the plates. He grabbed two cigars and handed one to Bob. He reached for two cut glass tumblers and changed his mind. He took a full bottle of Laphroaig and walked outside. He could hear Bob follow.

"Are you insane? We go this long and you start talking like that? Is this what you've become?"

Bob's eyes cast across the immaculate flower beds, erect blades of grass almost plump in their healthiness. The green carpet stretched in a pleasant undulation towards the cedar and the adjacent trout-filled pond.

"The only one insane is you, brother. I came up with the plan a lifetime ago in that shithole of a coffee shop we loved so much. You agreed. You didn't ask how I made so much money. You didn't want to. You loved the idea of sipping fancy drinks and talking high finance with those faggoty investment bankers. All dressed as though you people did anything. You are a glorified secretary. A cashier. A gofer." Bob pulled a lighter from his pocket and lit his cigar.

"I know you're angry."

"Angry? You go to the shopping mall to buy some jeans and you come out to find that someone has backed into your car. That makes you angry. I'm fucking incandescent with rage." He opened his mouth to speak, then thought otherwise. He spat on the grass instead.

Paul felt each word like a punch to his shoulder, chest, head. He lit his cigar to provide a physical barrier to his mouth from speaking.

"The silent treatment? We're not kids, Paul."

"I'm not ignoring you. I'm trying to light a cigar. I am digesting your accusing words. I feel like shit for you. I am feeling like a shit full stop." His body trembled as adrenaline took affect.

Bob's voice dropped in intensity in between long drags on his cigar. Smoke burst out of his mouth as he spoke. "I need to know if I still can count on you."

"Of course. What's mine is yours. Our deal stands."

"I'll need my half by the end of this week, latest."

"I told you I can't do that. Look around you. How can I turn this into cash?" Two rabbits dashed back into the underbrush as they approached.

"You're no fool, Paul. This is just the tip of the iceberg. You have cash stashed, you must have bonds and stocks that you and your City friends invested in. You forget that I know you better than anyone else. Possibly better than you know yourself."

Images flashed across Paul's mind. People. Meetings. Places. Things he would prefer unspoken. Forgotten.

"I don't have it. At least not that quickly. It would be suicidal on a number of fronts. Firstly, we would expose ourselves by moving that much just as you appear. Secondly, we would take a massive hit tax-wise and profit-wise if we liquidated such large positions. Ask me anything else. Push off your deal. Anything. I will not say no."

"You believe in your portfolio so much. You think it has real value. OK. You want me to walk away from my dreams so that you can keep your stability."

"Not mine. Ours. Don't you see how fragile everything is?" Paul spied a dead bough on an oak tree. He had asked for it to be cut long ago. He made a mental note to get it done.

"I'm an inconvenience now?"

"That's not what I said."

"I can't argue that you haven't been frugal, Paul. I can imagine that there are structures on structures with hidden get-away plans also set up. You can't unwind these without exposing yourself. I understand."

Paul nodded and puffed more contentedly on his cigar.

"Then what about me?"

"What do you want?"

"I need my life back."

"I can't give that to you."

"You can but you choose not to. It would be 'suicidal' according to you. But you could do it. It is a choice. You would rather not take any risk than honour our pact." Robert walked with a swagger, waving his arms as he spoke. They were close to the pond and the air quality changed. There was a faint smell of decomposing fish life.

"That's not fair, Robert."

"It is. You have no idea of the horrors that I had to face in that prison. Those weren't men. They were animals. I never felt fear in my life until then. Yet all of those horrors were fleeting. I knew they would pass. I knew that I had what no other person had."

Paul raised his eyebrows in expectation as Bob paused.

"You."

Paul looked away. That same tightness in his stomach followed by a cascade of electricity into his gut.

"I knew that I could bear anything because my brother would put me right. And here I am. Put me right."

"You want half, right? Why not live with me? Like old times. I'll unwind our positions slowly, shifting half of everything liquid into your name. Half of the real property we can resolve through adequate trust documents. You can live here or in any of the other properties we own. It's not bad, really."

"I'll be living your life."

"Our life. This is what we have. It is a long way from Winnipeg."

Bob walked in silence, smoke drifting behind him. Paul walked abreast, also in silence. A deer bolted from the underbrush as they unwittingly got too close for the Roe's comfort. Both followed it with their eyes and they were temporarily removed from the conversation at hand.

"Half of everything?" Bob repeated to himself as much as Paul.

"Yes."

"Half of *everything*?"

"Yes," Paul repeated. He wasn't losing anything. Half was always Robert's. Only now, it would be documented by more than a handshake.

"Then I will accept. The condition is simple. I will have half of everything you have managed to save us. Half of everything." He repeated.

"Sure. I'll set out everything for you and we can go over it later today." The bottle was unopened. Paul tore the metallic wrap off and uncorked it. He took a long drink, grimaced and handed it to his brother.

"To half of everything," Bob repeated before tilting back the bottle.

Chapter 13

The Derainier Estate, Sussex (May 2019)

Paul returned home, still unsure about what was happening. His call with Susan was odd. He needed to see his brother. Get his side. His hand grabbed the handle and the front door opened. His head cocked instinctively, listening for something. Probably primal, sensing a danger.

He walked in, noticed nothing out of the ordinary and headed upstairs. On the floor, blood. Drops, as though someone was moving. It came from his bedroom. He quickened his step and burst inside the master bedroom, just off the top of the stairs to the right. It commanded views of the entire property as it wrapped from the front to the back. His eyes scanned the room for immediate dangers then returned to the drops of blood that lead to the antique silk Tabriz at the foot of his bed. Mixed in the century's old masterpiece was a sludge of congealed blood. He wanted to prod it, then turned and followed the trail.

It led down the hall and up the stairs. His left hand and chest began to shake. He clenched his right fist and walked sideways, warily. His steps slowed, listening for any movement or sound. No staff. No Bob? No Susan.

As he was about to ascend the stairs, he heard a familiar voice.

"Lost?"

Paul turned around to see his brother grinning from a guest bathroom door ajar. His nose looked swollen and there were two paper projections out his nostrils.

"What the hell happened?"

"Nothing."

"Doesn't look like nothing."

"Did you talk to Susan?"

"Yep. She's pissed. More than I've ever seen her pissed."

"Did she say anything about me?"

"Not much. But I gather that you did something that pissed her off."

"Nothing that wasn't my due."

Part of Paul sank. Part of him asked blindly. "Due?"

"Just keeping to our deal." He turned to the mirror and touched his cheek gingerly.

"I'm trying not to make assumptions, Bob. You are going to need to spell it out to me."

Bob's hand froze in mid action, inches from his face, as he turned his head and locked eyes with Paul. "We agreed that I would get half of everything you have." He turned his head back and his fingers continued their prodding.

"I'm going to need to hear you say it." Paul's stomach turned on itself. His fingers became cold, and his tongue pushed hard against the roof of his mouth.

"She was asking for it. You know her. I may have said a few things. Harmless, really. She got all offended and kicked me in the balls, then face. I blacked out. When I came to, she was gone. Don't know where she learned to move like that. Back in the can, she would have been okay. No one would mess with that."

Paul's left hand was shaking harder than ever. His chest ached. His right hand was clenched tight. His muscles in his legs readied to launch. His breathing became slightly ragged.

Bob glanced down and smirked. His stance change was subtle. His arms hung loose by his sides, palms open. Ready.

Paul's breathing increased. His nails dug into the fleshy part of his palm. He moved his thumb, not sure where to put it. He remembered that you could break your thumb if you didn't close your fist right. His eye took in the frame between himself and Bob. His mind seamlessly overlaid Sun Tzu and Clausewitz as applied by armies and CEOs. It would take two Bobs to remove him from his fortified position. Paul, in the next instant, did a quick appraisal of his own physicality and let his fingers relax. There was no practical way in which he would be able to beat Bob physically in this current playing field. Best move: retreat, reassess, decide if frontal conflict was best route. He decided it wasn't.

"Did you touch her?"

"I really can't recall. I think I have a concussion." Bob touched his cheek for emphasis.

Paul was disgusted at his own cowardice. "Would you have touched her?" The words come out slowly, with more effort than he foresaw.

"We had a deal."

"Shut up with that nonsense. You can't add my wife into your mix. She's not some chattel."

"She's part of your life bought by our money in our partnership that I made. As you can't, or won't, let me have half of what is ours, you decided to let me share in half of everything."

"Yeah, I get it. Stop this shit. You've got my attention."

"Susan's part of the deal." Bob was smiling. His eyes sat staring coldly on a spot just below Paul's.

Paul's innards shrivelled. He wiped the sweat off his hands against his jeans. The fight was lost. In his mind, he retreated, preparing for his revenge. Strangely, he didn't feel as angry as he thought he should have.

One Month Later… June onwards, 2019 London and Greater London

The first night away was expected. Bob had acted despicably. Susan acted decisively. Paul, cowardly. There was no point looking for her, Paul thought. She would come back.

One week. Nothing apart from a terse call informing him that she was safe and would be in touch. Paul took advantage of the unexpected freedom and spent more time with Zara. There was a sense of relief. Why was he not jealous? Or angry? Or anything?

Two weeks. This was not a joke, he said to her recorded voice instructing him to leave a message and she'd get back to him. She didn't. He felt a pang. A dull ache that weakened his knees and sapped his resolve.

His brother was overwhelming. Susan was too stubborn.

Three weeks. Fear crept into his thoughts for the first time. She might want half of everything. Which everything? And Bob? Too much, too fast. Even Zara was changing. She was becoming clingy. Sentimental. He could feel her longing when they saw babies. He pretended to not see what they both knew was there. She wanted more. She saw no reason why Paul could say 'no' if his wife was gone. Paul worked the logistics of the problem.

Who or what was the real problem, he asked himself. The answer pointed to Bob.

How could he solve the problem? As he articulated the question, he shuddered at the cold that emanated within. The answer was unthinkable, so he put it out of his mind. What about Susan? She was mad and hurt. She would come back, he reasoned. Time would heal all.

One Month Later...
July, 2019
Derainier Estate, Sussex

Paul stared at a picture of himself in his high school yearbook. Tall, lanky, too much hair product, standing amongst his team mates. Each of them held a massive trophy, grinning at the camera. The caption explained that the team had a promising year but failed in the final stages. The props were hockey trophies of school teams that actually won something. It didn't seem to matter to those boys in the picture. They were having fun. They were young. The future was unlimited.

Each time he looked at this yearbook, he thought of big dreams of his father and family. The ease with which they talked about millions and tens of millions when they didn't have even a thousand to their collective names. It was his grades that got him out of there and fear that kept him away. Fear of becoming satisfied with mediocrity. Fear of losing the ability to dream.

Robert introduced him to Leo and their first deal that made money. Robert was the operator behind the scenes. Paul was the clean front man, and Leo was the financier. Lacking history, Paul was able to approach players who would never have sold to Leo. They gave the kid a chance. With Leo's backing, the kid won. Won big.

Jack, a developer, had built three hundred million dollars of property with immigrant investor funds. His investors got Canadian passports. He got their money. Eventually, his scheme unravelled and a hundred million dollars of his empire was available for the cost of the bank mortgage—fifty percent of the property value. If that piece could be digested, the rest was available. It was massive for Paul and Jack but just the right size for Leo. A plan was put in place, and executed to perfection. A once in a generation opportunity. Leo got the prize. Paul and Robert got their seed capital. After tax and expenses, just over two million bucks.

Paul remembered the feeling as he first received a bank statement with all those zeroes on the Royal Bank of Canada letterhead. His hands trembled as he opened the letter. He passed it to Robert who smiled wider than his usual Cheshire Cat imitation.

The two brothers did some more deals, but nothing so spectacular. They lost money when they tried to become money lenders. Neither was suited for that purpose and they decided to leave that element to solicitors in the future. Losses were offset by greater gains. Confidence was stratospheric and their conversation in Salisbury House was not long afterwards.

"What have I done by myself?" thought Paul. "Every transaction was set up by Robert and I was either the front man or the safe pair of hands. Can I be so foolish to have thought I was a participant? It was always Robert with me fitting into his plan, not the other way around."

He gazed across the pond as he sat under the Lebanon Cyprus tree on his Indian bench. The bottle was nearly done and he was on his second cigar.

"I'm left to talk to geese and squirrels," he said out loud to himself and his surroundings. He wished he could talk to someone. To share the burden and secrets he carried. The scotch had loosened his tongue and he felt that nature was trustworthy enough.

His words were slurred and his eyes drooped. The pain of living in a loveless marriage was only now hitting home. It was fine when he was sleeping next to Susan and sometimes with her. Cheating on her with Zara. Managing the financial portfolio for all of two hours a day.

Zara awoke in him a desire to come home. But home was not a place he desired to be. His emotions substituted Zara and he was happy for a moment. Until Zara was elevated to Susan and he was on the lookout for a replacement Zara.

"How did I become that letch?" He poured the rest of the bottle into his glass and exhaled deeply before drinking. He was tired of being a nobody. A no-one. Someone who had met somebodies. Leaders. People who made a difference, for better or worse. Someone who had realised that he was not one of those people.

"Then how can I even contemplate what I am trying so hard not to think about?" He finished his scotch, placed bottle and glass beneath the bench, and stretched out. There was no answer. If there was, he was unable to hear it. He was passed out on the ornate Indian wood carved bench.

He was shaken awake by a white-haired Indian wearing only a loincloth.

"Wha--!"

"Be calm, my friend. You are dreaming."

Paul was quiet, but not calm. This was not a dream. This was not a person he knew. Why was he in his home?

"Listen," the shaman said while turning his head towards the house.

Paul followed his gaze.

Screams, then a window opened. His window. Then items of clothing flew from the dark hole that was the window onto the ground below.

Paul blinked as it was no longer his estate outside of London but his family home in Canada. His mouth dropped when he saw his mother through the window, now no longer a dark void.

He was inside the room. His mother was young. And heavily pregnant. This was a dream, he thought.

His mother was screaming. Now they were downstairs. In the kitchen. She was wearing only a bra and panties. His father was there with his hands out. She was holding a large knife. Pointing the blade at her bulging stomach.

His father froze. She plunged the blade into her, screaming at a volume louder than Paul thought possible. The handle stuck out of her as she raised her bloodied hands as if in surrender, and fell to her knees.

They were in an ambulance, father with his head in his hands. Paramedics hunched over his mother. The knife handle still protruded from her. A yellow colour was painted around the blade. Her hands were strapped to her sides.

The operating room was a blaze of white light. Pictures of his mother's belly were on lit screens. His father was nowhere to be seen. The doctor and nurses were staring at another screen as the knife was slowly retracted from the belly. They were waiting for something.

The scalpel cut his mother's belly open, allowing the doctors to remove the baby and repair the damage. Remarkably, the knife missed the baby entirely apart from a small cut across the chest area.

Paul couldn't see the doctors or nurses. Just the sense of hands grabbing him, slapping him, making him cry. He opened his eyes to see the massive face of the birthing nurse. He looked down at his bloodied body, wrapped in a blue cloth. He would have laughed except he was crying already.

Paul felt a gentle hand and his eyes opened. It was green everywhere. The setting sun brought the shades of green alive all around him. Nettles, grass, rhododendrons, even the pond's grass at its edge and the lilies that floated held their own distinct colour of green.

He suddenly remembered and looked down to see his hands and adult self. He pulled up his shirt to see his birthmark—a red and white slash across his chest.

"What the hell are you doing now?" a familiar voice said, full of humour.

"Robert, I mean, Bob."

"You look like you've seen a ghost," His brother said with a smirk.

"Just a dream." Paul pieced his history from snatches of whispers as he grew up. He never quite lived it as his dream presented.

"More like a nightmare."

"What are you doing here?"

"I live here." Robert's Cheshire Cat grin parted his stubble to reveal flawless teeth.

"I mean, here. Now."

"Thought we should chat."

"Maybe tomorrow? I'm not in the right frame of mind."

"It's just that I've found something out and thought you should know."

Paul righted himself from his supine position and tried to focus his eyes on Bob.

"Ready? Ok. I've been following Susan and I know who she's with."

"Romeo Schmidt."

Bob stopped, mouth slightly ajar.

"And you found a new friend as well," Paul continued.

"How do you know this?"

"My wife disappears, presumably with a man. She's not talking to me. I am not a monster. I have feelings."

"You hired a PI," Bob finished. He laughed, slapping his chest and then Paul's shoulder. "I should have known."

"And your new friend?"

"Harmless. Likes being around power. Very malleable."

"What does he know?"

"What doesn't he know," Robert replied. "He knows more than he tells me. He thinks he is playing me."

Paul smirked. "If you are sitting at a game of cards and you can't figure out who the sucker is, you're it."

"Exactly."

Paul reached for the bottle and put it down lightly when he saw it was empty.

"Coffee?" Robert suggested.

"If you can throw in some dinner with it, absolutely."

Paul rocked forward and steadied himself on his feet. Bob stood patiently. The two brothers walked towards the house, their backs to the sunset.

Chapter 15

Eleven Months Later… Carnaby and Belgravia, London (June, 2020)

"I've always been a fighter, Paul." Robert was pacing. The two had just finished their lunch at Soho House and wanted to smoke desperately.

"We both know you have always been pugilistic." Noticing the agitation, Paul added. "What's wrong now? You look like you have ants in your pants."

"I know you like these places. Soho House is cool and Brad Pitt and actors come here, but there's no place to smoke a cigar."

"The world's become too healthy for you, Bob. But I agree. Let's find a place where there are no yoga mats or obviously healthy people listening to and fidgeting with their gadgets."

"You thinking where I'm thinking?"

"Not the club. Not today. How about the Boisdale? It's full of spooks, city boys, and men with mistresses."

"And they have a bar to kill for with a cigar terrace for degenerates like me. What are we waiting for?"

A short cab-ride later, they entered the all-red Boisdale. Walking distance to Victoria Station. A favorite with MI5 and security services. The game menu of venison and seasonal birds made it attractive to the shooters of the world. It was hard to find a place where a person who still enjoyed shooting and hunting could relax without feeling judged. The jazz, whiskey, and cigars rounded out the picture. Not elitist while attracting the most refined and educated of society, the Boisdale was a Scottish gem in the heart of London. It was after the lunch rush, not that there was any lunch rush during the pandemic, and they had most of the restaurant and all of the roof terrace to themselves. The humidor lacked Paul's favourite—Cohiba Siglio VI—so they went for a couple of Partagas Number 4's and a couple of monster Cuabas. The latter they doubted they would finish, but was worth it. They rarely saw the cartoonish cigar for sale and the quality, if real, was second to none.

"This is almost as good as it gets," Bob said as he exhaled. He started with the Cuaba. He put his feet on the chair across from him and splayed himself on the bench. Paul mirrored him, except that his feet were on the bench and he was sitting on the chair.

A bottle of Chateau Petrus 1995 sat on their table with some cheese that went untasted. An indulgent bottle of Auchentoshan Scotch (1978) sat next to it. Both brothers enjoyed large tumblers of the coppery-coloured liquid.

"Sticks to the teeth. Smooth and reassuring," Paul mumbled contentedly.

"The perfect complement to the Cuaba," Bob concurred.

The two sat for long moments in silence, enjoying the rare scotch as the celebrity Bordeaux Petrus aired patiently. A young woman with red hair and freckles wearing crème colored jodhpurs and riding boots walked in with a friend. They looked at the two middle-aged men, then looked at the labels of the bottles. They left before either Bob or Paul could catch their eye.

"It is the right thing to do," Bob said after they poured a second round into their heavy crystal glasses. He glanced around to ensure that there was no one else within earshot.

"Very desperate," Paul said.

"Insane. Unorthodox. Highly irregular, and illegal."

"We shouldn't even contemplate it."

"We'll lose a hundred million if we don't."

"Better to lose that than lose our liberty," Paul nodded knowingly to Bob. Bob winced.

"It's all on me. You don't need to know what I do or how I do it. Just that it needs to get done."

"We live in extraordinary times, brother."

"Amen to that. Just when you think you are rounding a corner, then BLAM. It's all over. Wait for the hit on the banks. It looks like they'll survive. The government is printing money like it's going out of fashion. All of this will need to be repaid."

"Taxes."

"Eventually. Debt now."

"But every debt has to be repaid eventually," Paul added.

There was a silence as the two puffed on their respective Cuabas. It was an hour and a half smoke. The shear nicotine hit on the system was mellowed by the scotch. It was like pressing the accelerator and brake on your car simultaneously.

"I have a guy."

"Do I need to know?" Paul asked.

"No. He used to be part of the Extinction Rebellion but he found them too tame. He wants to make a statement."

"And what statement is that?"

"Leave that to me. I need to establish a credible story before our properties start going up in flames. The last thing I want is to return to the can."

Paul's eyes closed as he worked through the logistics of the problem. He struggled to understand how he was even thinking like this. How could he allow himself to be led down this path? Things would be tight going forward. He may lose some money. But this plan may lead to him losing his liberty. Or worse. Yet he remained, listening to his older brother's plan. Trying to ensure that the empire didn't collapse under debt. His biggest concern was a collapse of value in commercial and retail property where he had leveraged himself to dangerous levels. There was an outside chance that he could lose everything.

His eyes opened to see the red-haired girl again. This time, she had three friends. All were relatively young, under thirty at least. They didn't look like hookers, not that either of the brothers would have found that offensive. Bob was especially fond of prostitutes as he felt it was an honest transaction. Before Paul opened his mouth, Bob invited them to sit with them. Two sat on either side of Bob, and the other two did the same on either side of Paul.

Paul watched as Bob sprang into action. Talking, motioning with his hands, smiling while waving at the waiter to bring more glasses. The girls were attentive and smelled intoxicating. The smell of a young woman or her hormones or the tight trousers and loose top made Paul forget he was married, separated, confused about Zara, and fearful of bankruptcy. Bob let the girls smoke the remains of his Cuaba. Paul, not wanting to look uncool, did the same. *So much for covid concerns,* Paul thought.

Six glasses of the Petrus were filled painfully slow by the sommelier. The bottle cost more than he made in a month. The girls took pictures of themselves and the brothers with the empty bottle and full glasses. The waiter took pictures of the girls kissing either side of the brothers' faces. A girl on each side with two very pleased men in the middle. Laughing and, soon, gentle touching made it feel natural. Paul shrugged as Bob ordered more. This time, two bottles of house champagne for the girls, he said. A selection of small bites were ordered to assist in the fun. Paul and Bob stuck to the whiskey. The red-haired girl leaned over to reach for the champagne, leg touching Paul's as she did. She left it there and refilled her and her friends' flutes. Paul could swear that he felt the fabric of her tight riding trousers through his own khakis. She said something to him. He couldn't be sure what it was. She picked up his whiskey tumbler and tasted it. Her lips made the slightest contact with the edge of the glass and she took a modest amount before returning it to him. When she opened her eyes onto him, he knew he was lost.

Derainier Estate, Sussex
July, 2020

The news hit Paul in unexpected ways. First, shock. His body felt waves of synaptic responses unsure of whether to push, pull, fire or be still. His muscles pumped full of blood, and adrenaline made him alert, then tired. His mind kicked in, analyzing the impact financially and practically. This part of him was pleased with the results. No divorce. No settlement. No more awkward situations. Finality. His conscience kicked in and was appalled at his callousness. How could he be so dismissive of the love of his life? Was it because he was incapable of love? Or that his love was never reciprocated?

The numbness continued for quite a period. He had to sit and drink something sweet. A tonic for shock. Through the numbness, he recalibrated his life. The only remaining stone in his shoe was Bob. He would deal with that in due course. Relief caused him more guilt and grief at Susan's plight. Relief at not having to face his own cowardice. Relief at not being subjected to a court-ordered accounting of his holdings.

"I need to go there," Paul whispered to Bob. He had called him back when his emotions settled.

"Sure thing. I'll meet you there. Your driver will take you?"

"Yeah. I'm getting in the car now."

An hour and forty-five minutes later, Paul decided to walk the remaining distance. Park Lane and the surrounding blocks were cordoned off. There were police, ambulances, helicopters and firetrucks. Reporters and cameras were respectful in the early moments, collaring officers to get the latest news. Tourists were few and far between during the pandemic so it was primarily locals who stood and gawked at the flames and cacophony of the moment. Bob met his brother at the cordon. Bob must have made arrangements in anticipation, because the officer ushered the two in and walked them to the command post of the fire service. Once inside, no one took notice of them.

"Were there any survivors?" Paul asked. His face was drawn from strain and the beginning stages of grief.

"More than I thought," Bob replied. "Not enough." He added.

"Have they found them?"

"Not yet. The flames are coming under control but some parts are going to need to burn out. They are protecting the surrounding buildings from contagion at this stage."

"Do they know what caused it?"

"Too early to tell," Bob lied. He suspected but never expected something like this. And definitely not with his sister in law.

"What can we do?"

"Truthfully?"

"No. Tell me a fucking lie." Some color rose in Paul's otherwise grey pallor.

"We find a bar. Get drunk. Maybe we go to the club."

"I need to wait here a bit longer."

"Paul." Bob placed his hand on his brother's shoulder. "If they find her, they won't be able to immediately identify her," he said softly.

Paul bowed his head and Bob felt a short silent sob.

"I can't go. I'll wait. Even if it is for nothing."

"I'll wait with you…"

The air was thick with the smell of burnt rubber and garbage. The front of the hotel had collapsed amidst screams from onlookers. Paul and Bob stood stoically. Sirens could be heard in the distance and up close. Neither brother took notice of the sounds. Sensory overload reduced them to avatars of minds that refused to engage.

As time passed, ambulances arrived and left. These were the sights not shown on television, Paul thought. The body bags. The somber medical examiners. There was chatter that survivors and relatives should contact the police on a dedicated number/website. Bob did the necessary and put his phone away. Paul was unable to focus on any task. His guilt and relief and grief swirled inside him, making him unable to function.

Chapter 16

Marylebone, London (July, 2020)

"It all started with Zara, didn't it?" Paul was slumped over his third double whiskey sour at the club. Bob sat next to him. They were in a separate room from the main reception. It was lined with bookshelves, full of leather bound books. The books didn't look inviting, being almost too perfect to disturb. The oxblood leather armchairs, a staple in every corporate office last century, held the two big men comfortably.

"Are you sure?"

"Well, maybe there were a few others. Maybe she thought I didn't fully commit."

"You think?" Bob said the words before he could curate his thoughts fully.

Paul looked up sharply. "I wouldn't cast stones if I were you." His voice held a needle of aggression looking for a target.

"I never said I was a saint and I definitely didn't hold myself out as being a family man. Quite the contrary, I would say."

Paul was too much in shock to care. His anger subsided as he cradled his oversized whiskey tumbler. The ice clinked against the glass. "Do you think they'll have all the bodies out today?" His stomach tightened at the image that passed through his mind. There was nothing left to come out of his stomach if it did rebel against him again, apart from the most recent whiskey sour.

"Don't worry. I've got a guy who'll contact me. Everything's taken care of." Bob lifted his chin as a woman looked in on them. He lifted two fingers and she nodded.

"Anything else?" she asked, knowing what 'anything else' meant in the Club.

"Anything else?" Bob asked Paul, eyebrows raised.

"No. Thanks, anyway." Paul wanted to be alone with his brother. To feel the pain wash over him. He couldn't get past the guilt that he had something to do with Susan's death. That if he just loved her. But he did. Does. If he just was faithful. He was. Partly. But, it was her fault as well, he reasoned. She didn't return his love. Or, maybe, he shouldn't have been sharing his attentions with others. Or, maybe, that's what life is.

All a bunch of shit mistakes and petty grievances. The temporary becoming the permanent.

"You okay, bro?" Bob didn't like the look in his brother's eyes. He'd seen it in prison just before someone topped themselves. "You look like you have the whole world on your shoulders. It's not your fault, okay? Accidents happen."

"This wasn't an accident. Some asshole blew up the hotel."

"Yes, but it was an accident that she was there when it happened."

"And why was that weirdo friend of yours hanging out with them anyway? What's his deal? Why do any of you want to be with him? He's a loser. A follower. Probably dangerous."

"He's fine. Wouldn't hurt a puppy. I befriended him to get to know what your wife's up to. I got to know him. He's been through a lot. A bit damaged. From what I've seen, he is a loyal friend."

"Great. I don't like it that he just happened to be with them when this accident happened."

"He told us about her being in there. The only reason he isn't under rubble is he wanted to let them be alone."

"So he says." Paul was grumpy.

A mid-twenties young woman in a tight black dress came in with a silver tray and two drinks. She placed one next to each man. Paul's eyes followed the curve of her hip as she bent slightly. His hand reached out and gently traced the fabric from her waist to her knee. She smiled and turned her face towards him, hair slightly tousled and hanging down. It created a powerful frame for her face. She said something and Paul nodded. She walked behind his chair and put her hands on his neck and shoulders. He closed his eyes as she began to massage. She rubbed his ears gently, following the curvature of his jaw and skull with her fingers. Pressing firmly to starve the muscles of oxygen followed by the release. The muscles filled with blood and relaxed. Using this technique, she worked her way along his head to his neck. She followed the spine and then back up to the large muscles connecting the shoulder and neck. Back into the neck and skull. Back into the spine.

Paul relaxed and let his eyes droop. He took off his jacket to free up access. Her fingers were strong. Certain. There was a very subtle hint of perfume as her hair brushed along his face on occasion. At first he thought that she did it on purpose. He felt himself sink further into the chair. His body giving over. The tension giving way to the personal attention of this woman without a name. He refused to ask her name. He didn't want to know.

She asked him something again and he nodded his head. She came around and extended her hand. He put his hand in hers, dreamlike. She led him to one of the rooms with the promise of a full massage. He tried to look back but his brother was no longer in the adjoining chair. He must be sleeping. He let the dream unfold.

Chapter 17

Aftermath

Paul woke slowly, as was his habit. He had enjoyed affluence for long enough to plan his days according to his needs and wants as opposed to other people's schedules. Mornings were all about allowing the body to transition from a restorative hibernation to living life. Today was different as he awoke in a strange bed. The sheets were of the finest quality, similar to the ones he had when he stayed at the Fairmont Hotel in Montreux, Switzerland. The pillows were huge and stuffed just enough to hold his head exactly as his head wanted. He was naked, which was unusual. He preferred to wear something to bed as he got aroused easily without clothes. His arms extended as he tensed his muscles, arching his back and feeling… what? A body next to him. Also naked. His memory kicked in and he knew where he was and what he had done.

He sat up in bed.

The figure with her back to him sensed his movement and her breathing altered. She pushed herself next to him. He ran his hand along her shoulder, down her back, and down her thigh. Young. He was reminded of what she did to him last night. He wanted a massage. She gave him the best massage he could remember. Then, the best sex. It wasn't love. It wasn't a lay. It wasn't purely mechanical. It was artistry and both he and his body appreciated the talent that went into the experience. He startled as these thoughts passed through his mind. He could finally understand why Bob went there.

On the side table was the remains of an expensive bottle of burgundy and the regular scotch that he drank. It had the cork in it as the smell was too much for some. He liked his scotch to be anywhere from 18 to 25 years old. Many said that it didn't matter once it was bottled; spirits didn't age once bottled. The key was in the aging process. The sherry oak barrels, the thousand things and nothings that made the difference between a decent and an excellent bottle. He didn't bother about the details. He enjoyed the intensity.

His head won the deliberations and he grabbed the sparkling water instead.

He jolted when he went back to why he was at the club. Susan. Most likely dead. No phone messages that she was alive. By her or the police. Or Bob.

He settled into the pillows and let his fingers play with his lover's hair, waking her in the process. She turned and smiled at him. He reflexively smiled back. She moved her warm body alongside his and felt him respond. Paul remained where he was and nodded imperceptibly. She seemed to read his mind and began kissing him gently. First, on the lips, then neck, shoulders, and chest. Her hands traced his legs and thighs. Her mouth, his torso. Paul's mind wandered as she pleasured him. Part of him expected this level of personal service. It was not hedonistic if they both consented? If they both enjoyed?

He had become that person, he thought with no malice. Just acceptance. He took what he wanted. He was lucky, and any business person would tell you that it was better to be lucky than smart. Lucky in getting out of that small town. Lucky in being the safe pair of hands with Bob taking all the risks. Lucky even with Susan dying. She would have taken half of everything. If she could find it. But it was all tied together. Once one started pulling on a string, it would all unravel. He hadn't fully fortified himself yet.

A gasp escaped him and a couple of low breaths as the pressure in him began to build. She was good. Zara was nothing compared to this. Hell, he couldn't even remember the girl's name. From that moment on, Paul vowed that he would never be so foolish as to marry again. Or make himself vulnerable to the confiscatory laws of matrimony, common law or otherwise. He would find artists like the one he was with.

With Susan gone, he had only one threat to his existence. The thought had entered his head before but was dismissed just as quickly. It entered again. He reached over and poured himself a scotch. His breathing increased, shudders interspersed as his body began to twitch in anticipation. He tried to think about Bob. He drank back the scotch and looked at the ceiling. It seemed natural as his body strained against the stimulation.

There was only one solution for Bob. He wanted half of everything. It was unreasonable. Paul refused to allow his mind to accept what was being asked of it. In order for Bob to not get his fair share, he must not be able to accept his fair share. Paul thought of Bob in the Dorchester. Blown to bits in a freak act of terrorism. Why couldn't he have been there with Susan. Then all his troubles would be over. His life would be simplified and he could live out his days without the drama and threats.

His mind could no longer hold a thought as his legs and torso seized up, pulsing in readiness. Willing the release. His hands grabbed at the bedding, clenching. His head rocked listlessly as his eyes rolled to the back of his head. His mouth became dry and his breathing was ragged. It started as a tremor. The shaking began as every muscle in him tensed. Her art delivered him to a new high.

When the moment came, he released a tension he didn't believe he had. In that moment, all grief and pain from the loss of Susan and Bob washed away. He lay on his back, propped by the sumptuous pillows, as the artist raised her head and pulled her hair from her face. She was smiling. Youth. Energy. Hope.

His answer.

Fourteen Months Earlier… Robert Derainier, aka Bob Day (May 2019)

Robert Derainier glanced out the window of his Delta Air economy seat as the pilot ordered all flight crew to take their seats. Final descent. The words seemed appropriate, Robert thought. Food tray up, window blind up, seat up. He could feel the soft flesh of the potpourri scented woman next to him as her folds of skin breached both the space above and below the armrest. Her arm was bare and her sweat was being soaked up by his fleece. The thought made him shudder. She had defiled one third of his entire wardrobe. The other two thirds lay in a carry-on stored in the overhead compartment. He hadn't the time or the money to go shopping after prison. At least his brother hadn't forgotten him or the reason why he was in prison. The ticket was waiting for him as soon as his probation officer said it was okay to go. Prison time was hard and he did things and had things done to him that he would rather forget. But the purgatory of probation officers feigning interest in his well-being while he struggled to survive in an underpaying stock-taking job almost broke his patience.

The plane landed without incidence and Robert waited for the other passengers to get up, stand, grab their bags and then wait because they were in the back of the plane and 300 other people needed to deplane before they were able to move. Ms. Potpourri squeezed out and he sat until the entire rear section was clear apart from the air crew who smiled and bad farewell to their latest round of passengers. *What must they think of us*, Robert mulled as he grabbed his single carry-on bag and turned sideways to make his way down the corridor. He was a big man, over 6 foot 4 inches, probably well over 220 pounds but blessed with genetics in that this was mostly muscle. His shoulders were square if not protruding from all of the gym work. He retained the open face that people trusted and the piercing blue eyes that disarmed even the most recalcitrant mark. Even his slightly receding hairline was forgiven when he smiled. He smiled at each of the air stewardesses and noted that he still had what it took. He could tell when a woman was interested.

All of that nonsense would need to wait until he resolved matters with his brother. Paul was a good man.

He trusted him and still trusted him now. But the last five years had made Robert, now just Bob, a bit less sure of people. For ease of internet searches stumbling across his past, he changed his last name to Day. Bob Day was a middle aged man of athletic build who was looking for investors for his latest venture. This would be the angle he would take with Paul.

Airport security was a little tougher than he remembered, but nothing like the chaos after 9/11. 2019 provided a smooth functioning system of body, bag, and random searches ranging from wands to full body scans. Landing had almost no security. Just passport control. He held his breath for a moment as the border guard ran his passport through the scanner. He didn't have the biometric passport which might have allowed him to go through with a machine as his toll master. Then again, they probably didn't allow US citizens that privilege yet.

"I have family in the UK," Bob said in response to the query of not having any luggage apart from a carry on when travelling internationally. He looked at the young border guard with his stab vest and stern face and thought about Paul. Fifteen seconds later, he was turning the corner and looking for the exit and into the airport where he assumed Paul would be waiting.

"Robert!" The voice was followed by Paul.

"Good to see you, Paul. A bit of a brutal flight. Was hoping for an upgrade, but I appreciate it wouldn't have looked very good."

"Not yet." Paul looked around and grabbed his brother's bag. "Do you want something to eat? A coffee?"

"How about a two-hour steam and massage followed by a three star Michelin meal?"

Paul looked at him from the side as they dodged people. He paid for the parking and went across to the carpark.

"Gloria, sorry, our housekeeper is making something nice tonight and you are staying with us until we come up with a plan. I think we can get you some hands on treatment but, please, nothing in the house. Susan will cut off my balls if you did."

"From what I gather, she probably is already sharpening the scissors."

"Ha. Why do you say that?"

"You're too confident, Paul. I haven't seen you in over five years, and you look great. No married man looks that happy unless he's got something on the side."

Paul reddened but didn't say anything. "You have a one-track mind, Robert."

"It's Bob, now. Bob Day."

"I guess it's better than Bob Hope. Am I still your brother?"

"Only to Susan and those we can't avoid telling. If you don't mind."

"Understood."

"And we will need to speak about you know what at some point as well."

Paul was silent. He didn't expect this so soon. "Of course. Let's get you sorted and then we'll talk strategy."

"Politicians talk strategy. Generals talk logistics." Bob jumped into the passenger seat of his brother's Vogue and began putting the seat back, eyes closed.

Paul started the engine and pulled away slowly. His mind was working out logistics.

Chapter 19

Derainier Estate, Sussex (May, 2019)

As the car slowed in silence in the mid-morning sun, Paul gave Bob a nudge.

"Wake up, we're here."

Eyes still closed, Bob reached down and to the side of his seat to find the controls. The sleep that eluded him on the plane embraced him on the hour and half ride from Heathrow to Paul's home. He opened his eyes as they began the mile-long approach to the house. The road curved through ancient woodland, the last of the bluebells just visible to a trained eye. Bob's eye surveyed as an owner, not botanist.

"Nice place you've got here." No trace of jealousy or irony.

"One of King Henry VIII's shooting retreats. The lodges have been long torn down but there is an Elizabethan manor not far from here that still remains. The rest of the buildings are mainly Victorian."

Bob took in the centuries old Lebanese Cyprus trees, Sequoias, and landscaped grounds. "Hard to imagine it being designed better than this," he said.

"I had nothing to do with it. It has evolved over five centuries. All I did was resurface the road and modernised the electrics and plumbing of the houses and pool."

"Nice." Bob said as much to himself as his brother. "Quite a difference from where I just spent the last five years."

Paul was silent. There was nothing he could say to that. Instead, he reached out and squeezed his older brother's shoulder in solidarity. They both nodded, mirroring each other's deepest feelings without speaking.

There were two cars in the circular drive that housed a fountain and bronze statue of a dancing woman. Paul raised his eyebrows and shrugged his shoulders when he saw an expectant look from Bob.

As they exited the car, they heard before saw the guests. The door to the kitchen was open and sounds of laughter and loud talking punctuated the silence. Only the engine ticked, or maybe it was the metal cooling, providing a reminder of their journey. Bob grabbed his solitary bag and started towards the sound. All tiredness was gone. His senses in overload, he tried to take in everything at once.

"Hi, sis," he said with a grin as he opened his arms to hug Susan. She, in turn, backed herself against the kitchen cabinets and allowed him to give her a quick hug and peck on the cheek. "Who are your friends?"

"This is Candace," she started.

Bob went over and gave her a massive hug, almost lifting her off the floor. As he placed her back down, he gave her bum a firm but deliberate pat. Candace's eyes opened, then shot a glance at Susan and, then, Pepe.

In reply, Pepe stuck his hand out to greet the stranger. "Hi. I'm Pepe, Candace's husband." He looked at Bob fully in the eye and held his hand. It was no longer a greeting. He leaned in and spoke so that just Bob could hear. "And if you ever do that again, I'll smash in your pretty smile." His grip was like steel and his eyes opened slightly as he said it, nose flaring perceptibly.

Bob held the stare and grip. He had been working out but was still surprised at the strength. He was two inches taller than Pepe and probably thirty pounds of muscle heavier. After a full second longer than required, he voluntarily relaxed his hand and felt Pepe do the same. He laughed. "I like you, man. Finally, someone with some balls. Oh, and sorry. Candace, is it? I didn't mean anything by it. I try to stop but, habits, you know."

Candace, flushed and angry that Pepe intervened the way he did, nodded her acceptance of Bob's apology. Part of her liked a man that took charge. After the anger, she found her body warming. Despite her education, feminism, and worldliness, she got turned on by men fighting over her. Pepe, she decided, would get a treat tonight.

"Wine, Robert?" Susan was trying to diffuse the situation. *He always created a scene*, she muttered to herself.

"It's Bob, thanks. That would be great."

"Have you eaten?"

"It feels like that's all I've been doing but I could have a bite if you're already making."

"What time zone are you on? It's not even noon yet and you're into wine?" Candace was trying to ignore his earlier behaviour and try to help out Susan. She had been warned about him from her.

"It's noon somewhere, sweetheart. Sorry, I mean Candace. It's been a while since I've been in polite company."

"Where you've been?" Pepe asked.

There was a silence and Paul piped in. "He's been travelling on business with roughnecks. You know how those oil guys are. Worse than Marines, I'm told. Isn't that right, Bob?"

"Uh huh. Roughnecks. Felt like I was in prison. Couldn't wait to get away."

"Yeah," said Pepe. "Like prison but without the gang rape, eh?" He was smiling and accepting wine. Susan was pouring and determined to get everyone drunk as quickly as possible. No one seemed to mind.

"Yeah," Bob replied. His eyes looked past the crowded kitchen to the family of deer that delicately stepped across the lawn in the distance.

"Well, I'm sure Bob is tired and would like to get some sleep," Paul interrupted.

"I'm fine. I'll try to blast through a few more hours—and drinks, thanks Susie—before crashing. Hopefully I'll sleep through 'til tomorrow morning and all will be well."

"Good luck on that," Susan said.

The second hand of the clock was heard as the group momentarily realised that everything they could say had been said.

"How about this weather," Candace asked no one in particular.

"Yeah, really spectacular. Speaking of which. Paul, do you think you have time to walk me through some of your gorgeous gardens? The rest of you wouldn't mind, would you?" Bob's blue eyes beamed innocence as he met each pair in return. "You wouldn't have a spare cigar, Paul? It's been ages since I had a good smoke."

Paul nodded, retrieved three cigars from his humidor and handed one to Pepe and Bob while putting his in his shirt pocket. The two brothers left through the side door, past the potting room, neither of them commenting on the earthy smells of the peat and compost or the burst of colours. It was Susan's favourite room and pastime.

"That was quite a show you put on in there," Paul said when they were sufficiently far away.

"Hardly. I actually thought the girl was a present for me. I wasn't going to look a gift horse in the mouth. Who would have thought that she was married to some skinny bloke with fuzzy pubic hair on his head? Just look at her. I bet she gets whatever she wants, doesn't she?"

"Candace is a respected doctor and a really nice person. Yes, she does know how to dress to turn heads. But that may be as much our issue as hers. I take her for what she is. Nice to talk to, nice to look at, and an amazing friend of Susan. They are almost inseparable."

"All I can say, that guy is one lucky sonofabitch. It makes me want to find some more than ever. She turned on a switch inside me. Paul, you don't know what it's like. Five years. I mean, five fucking years of only your hand to keep you company. I thought I was pretty civil, all things considered."

Paul let it pass. They walked in silence. Bob pulled his cigar and Paul passed the clipper to him. He watched as his brother butchered the end before handing it back to him. Paul cut his deftly, his expertise borne out through experience. They lit their cigars standing, allowing the flame to take hold before slowly continuing their stroll.

"When can I get it?" Bob said after almost five minutes in silent reverie.

"It's not that simple and you know it."

"It *is* that simple and you know it. I want my half and I want it now. You knew I was coming here. There was only one reason I had to come here in person."

"I know but I thought you'd listen to reason."

"Reason? Five fucking years. That's all the reason I have or know. I want it and I need it."

"Look around, Robert. Everything we have is in assets. Nothing is liquid. It had to be done this way."

"Then undo it. Enough time has passed. Everything and everyone has moved on. It's ancient history."

Paul stepped over a fox hole and half-jumped across a shallow ditch-cum-stream. Bob did the same. In doing so, they strolled from the woods to the open pastures. There were no sheep on it yet.

"It would need time."

"I don't have time."

"How long before you need it?"

"Yesterday."

Paul paused, using his cigar as an excuse not to reply immediately.

"That's not possible," he said finally.

"Paul. You know what we did. What I sacrificed. I am asking you to now fulfil your end of the deal. If you feel a little pain, believe me it will be a lot less than anything I had to endure."

The brothers shared the large muscular athletic build of their father. It was easy to see that they were brothers. In the field, they walked shoulder to shoulder, heads bowed in thought and quiet talk. Bob, the elder, walked with the confidence of a man of action. He thought, decided, and did. Paul walked with the determination of a philosopher. He thought, recalibrated, and thought some more. Rarely did he make a decision. His world was one of shades, not absolutes. Amidst the tannins, heated saliva, and smoke, he searched for a solution.

"How much do you really need?" Paul asked.

"£30 million," Bob replied without hesitation.

Paul's body felt the impact of the words before his brain. He felt the shake in his hands and the dropping sensation in his torso. It was an impossible sum.

"That's too much."

"It's what I'm owed. It is more than fair."

"How do you figure? I had costs. It wasn't easy. I had to pay a lot to secure it. Do you know how hard it was to end up with what we have? Clean, no questions, no investigations."

"You had your costs. I had mine. You and I both know that £30 million is fair. I need it to make my next move."

"Which is?"

"You want in?"

Paul shook his head. "Nope. I'm out. I've got enough."

"Then you don't need to know. Just find me my money." He took a final puff of the cigar and tossed it onto a mole hill before crushing both with the heal of his shoe.

Chapter 20

Tipping Point

"Candace, I'm horrified. Sorry about that." Susan took two steps towards her friend before she was stopped by two palms facing her.

"No problem, really. You think I've never had to deal with assholes before?"

"I should have warned you more than I did, that's all. I was more concerned about myself. I never thought he'd try it on with you."

"I noticed your technique. Well done. Backing up against the furniture. I've taken note and will try it next time."

"Hey, that's BS and you know it," Pepe joined it. "He's got no right to do anything like that. I was ready to pop him one."

"I know, sweetheart. And I love you for it. But you forget that women deal with that every day in every walk of life. You may have just seen a slice of it today."

"You know I'm a bit better than that, Candy. I guess I expect it in a bar or some macho sporting event, not a kitchen in a conservative province in the UK."

"Pepe's right, Candace. We shouldn't have to put up with it. But we do because we are pragmatists and it is still socially acceptable. When he first did it to me, I said nothing. The next time, he left his hand there for quite a bit longer than necessary."

Sensing a shift in the conversation, Candace's eyebrows furrowed and lips pouted. "Susan, that's not cool. That's way over the line. Did you talk to Paul about it?"

Susan straightened her shirt briskly, brushing off invisible crumbs, and rubbed her neck. "Let's just say he didn't do a Pepe. He was all conciliatory and apologetic and understanding."

"But did nothing."

"Yeah. Fuck all." Her head scanned the counters, looking for an opened bottle. "It did something to me. I was so in love with him, we had recently married and bought this beautiful home. There was nothing I could fault him with. I accepted everything he said and pushed it down deep. Perhaps today is the day it comes out." She poured herself a large red and indicated whether either of the two wanted some. They both did.

"Not sure what to say, Susie. That sucks."

"Yep. Big time."

"So is that the moment that you point to when you look back on your relationship with Paul?" Pepe said.

Both women looked at him as though they just realised he was there.

"Yes. Yes, it is. When I look at when things started going the wrong direction, that was the moment. A million little things since, but that was the first. The proverbial thin edge."

"There hasn't been anything more?" Candace asked.

"No. Not at all. And even that was a long time ago."

"Yet you still protect yourself now."

"Yeah. It was a violation. It is a violation. It will always be a violation. And he gets away with it."

"Guys like that tend to. Good looking, confident, smart. One of the boys. There's something about him that I can't put my finger on. It is as though he's been hardened. Toughened more than he needed to be. And I'm not talking about an over-enthusiastic personal trainer."

"He's got a history," Susan said. "It's not mine to tell or tattle."

"Aww, you can't say that and then shut up! Spill it." Candace had moved closer and now rubbed her shoulder against her friend's.

"Another time. I've already said too much. Forget everything. I don't think we need to be here when they're back. Let's say we go to town and get some lunch?"

"Town as is the local gastro-pub down the lane or London town and a three star Michelin?"

"Chubby tyre mascot guy type of lunch."

"The usual?"

"I'll call and reserve. You see if Gloria's husband is available to drive us in. I don't think any of us are in any shape."

Susan left the kitchen and went upstairs into the master bedroom where she dialled in the reservation. She replayed the image of Pepe moving into Robert's personal space menacingly and whispering his warning just loud enough for Robert to hear—but still heard by her. The strength, the sinew of his arms as he motioned, the absurdity of the action. All made her think of Romeo and his single-minded strength. Romeo was tall, like Pepe, but that was where the comparison ended. Romeo was the best of Brad Pitt and Leo DiCaprio, confident and handsome but not pretty. A man. She thought of him touching her. She put it out of her mind, but he came back. The more she pushed him away, the more omnipresent in her mind he became. It was ridiculous. They met in a café and bumped into each other on the pavement. There was nothing more.

And yet.

She picked up her phone and called his number.

"Hi. It's me. Susan, we met... yes, exactly. I'm going to be in town for lunch and wouldn't mind if you could find some time for me after that, say, 4 o'clock?

Formal? No, just thought we'd continue that conversation. Oh, you can't. OK, I understand. No problem. Maybe some other… you can? When? Where? Sorry, did I hear you correctly? OK. But that is sounding weird. Yes, this call to you is also a bit weird, so we're even. … OK. Thanks. Will do. See you then."

When she pressed end, her hands were shaking slightly and more than a little sweaty. She could feel her pulse in her fingers and neck.

It felt wonderful.

Chapter 21

Park Lane, London (May 2019)

Lunch at Le Gavroche was spectacular. It was Candace's go-to place and became Susan's after her first visit. They went for the taster menu with paired wines. Off Park Lane, around the corner from the Dorchester, this gem of a restaurant was a perfect coupling of establishment English charm and French culinary mastery. The red décor, intimate tables, and attentive wait staff. The three hours passed in laughter, a couple of tears, and general bonding of the three friends. Pepe had made himself an equal amongst the two strong-willed women. He joked that he could be their gay friend but Candace said that was impossible. It was warming to Susan to see the genuine love and affection the two had for each other. It made it easier for her to bade them farewell after lunch and make her way to Romeo, a little later than expected.

"You look content with yourself," he greeted her with a swift kiss on either cheek. She caught a hint of his cologne and she wondered when she would be confronted with the part of him she couldn't tolerate. For some reason, he was wearing a rucksack on his back.

"I'm a contented gal," she said before she could stop herself. Part of her slapped her forehead for such a pubescent reply.

Romeo smiled and offered her his hand. She took it gently.

They walked in silence for a period of time before Susan asked, "you were a little suspicious earlier today and I really didn't want to ask about the turtle on your back, but…"

"I know," he laughed. "It was a bit cloak and dagger. And I'm a bit mad to be doing this in daylight. Damn these long days. I think this would have been better to implement November onwards."

Susan raised her eyebrows but said nothing.

"Promise to not say anything about this? I know we've barely known each other but I'm an all or nothing person. Either you'll understand or this will be the last time we see each other."

Susan's stomach tightened. His hand was dry and firm. No callouses. A paper pusher of some sort, whatever his story. She would hear him out. She gave a slight squeeze of his hand but said nothing.

"I'm pissed off," he began. "Pissed off with myself, my family, my town, country, society, the world. You name it, I'm pretty unhappy with the way things are being run or the trajectory of where it is going. True, this is nothing new. Every adolescent is angry. All of us come up against barriers that define and direct us. Like walls in one of those experimental rat mazes. Eventually we aren't even aware that there are walls that are stopping us from going forward. All we know is that there is no forward, backwards, left or right. All we have is what is given to us. Our world is curated from cradle to grave. We are the product of centuries of enlightened thought, war, economic highs and lows, and the resultant social experimentations by the great and good. We are barely aware of the path that came before us and how it has paved our present and future."

Susan tried to not roll her eyes. This was amateur stuff. Nothing more than first year university ravings in the social club by the stereotypical philosopher or bad boy talking to his mates or chatting up a girl willing to listen. It was a good thing he was such a looker, she reminded herself.

"To cut across the ramblings, I know, I am not being eloquent or profound. What I have discovered is that I think there may be a role for a radical gadfly in post-modern civilisation. Not the type that sits on books in an ivory tower. One that is on the ground, with the citizens, demanding more. There is nothing wrong with being an academic. Everything that has come before is the result of academics. But also enlightened people with money and time to grapple with the important issues of existence. How we earn money, distribute money, how much should we allow the rich to accumulate, how poor should we allow the poor to get, and so on. The academics feed ideas into the thought universe and people graduate having debated the finer points of each academic view. It works, it is sound, and it is sustainable. Unfortunately, an apathy has taken hold of the masses. We are fed and are entertained. Bread and circuses. It is a tried and true formula."

Susan couldn't hold her tongue any longer. "And you plan to wake the masses."

"In a word, yes."

"With a cattle prod?"

"Carrots are just more food. I am opting for the stick."

"And which dictator do we entrust with this power?"

"None. It must be grass roots."

"But a leader always emerges, and many times not the way you think. Unintended consequences and all that."

"Yes. True. It may come to that. But I cannot sit back and do nothing."

"You think you can change anything? Are you going to run for office? Become Prime Minister?" She flashed a smile at him as she said it. If he wasn't an American, she could see it happening.

"No interest in becoming a politician. I don't think I'd be any good at it. It is a far too important job to be given to populists. They are our elected voice to get our will done."

"But you are saying that our will is not being done."

"Exactly."

"So what's the big plan, Romeo?" She was still holding his hand. They had walked from Brent Cross Shopping centre in North West London onto the flyover bridge for cars. There was a pavement for them to walk alongside it. He had stopped and was gazing over the sea of cars travelling in four lanes either way.

"As you know, this is the North Circular. It is one of the busiest A-roads in the UK. It allows for the movement of workers in their cars, busses, trucks to get from A to B in London because the side roads are single lane and could never carry the level of traffic. Emergency services, essential services also use these roads. It is like a body's artery."

Susan didn't like where this was heading. She became wary of the bag on Romeo's back. She looked where she could run to in the event that he planned to blow himself and the bridge up. She tensed and pulled her hand towards herself.

"I'm not doing anything too insane," he said, sensing the change of atmosphere. "I am trying to wake everyone up." He took off his rucksack and put it on the pavement, next to the railing.

"You are starting to scare me," Susan said, taking a step backwards.

Romeo put his hand down and out, palms up. He stood with his legs apart and looked at her. "I am not going to do anything violent. I'm not blowing anything up. I'm not killing anyone. I just want to demonstrate in a way that will do something."

Susan's heart raced, palms sweating as she cursed her schoolgirl behaviour. What educated woman of the world meets a stranger, maybe a strange man, in a parking lot and walks onto a bridge spanning a heavily travelled motorway. After only meeting him, really.

She watched him bend down and begin to unzip the rucksack. She looked the length of the flyover. They were in the middle. It would take too long for her to reach the end before the blast hit her. She was dead. She could see Candace and Pepe and the fifteen courses of food that they absorbed in such frivolity earlier that day. Not a care in the world. All the history of Candace's family, of her own violent brush with death in Umhlanga, dear Sable her saviour not being around to vet this strange man. It was too fast. She hadn't really loved anyone since Marcel. Why was she still with

Paul? She wanted to end it. Hell, she was here with Romeo because she wanted to end it. She hadn't done anything with her life since Marcel. Just floating along on her looks and money. Both would run out. Just not today. Not now. Not like this. She closed her eyes and prepared for her body to be ripped to pieces, unidentifiable to all but forensics who didn't even see her parts. Just pieces of meat or DNA they gathered from the edges of the blast site if she was lucky. Not unlike the suicide bombers who left body parts in trees. Those news pieces never talked about those nasty elements. Too real. Too visceral. In violation of the large networks and large IT companies' policies—whatever those were. Unless those images passed the curators' approval, the masses would not see it. Modern day censors.

Her body squeezed itself shut, taking in every sound, smell, and movement in ultra-slow motion. She heard the individual teeth on the zipper as he opened the rucksack. She heard a rustling of something and then the smell his cologne as he came near her. Her body jumped as she felt his hand on her shoulder, gently. She realised he was talking to her. Quietly, reassuringly, like a tamer of wild horses. She opened one of her eyes slowly. He was holding something in his hand in front of her.

"Touch it, if you want," he said. "The whole ruck-sack is full of them."

She put her hand out tentatively, knowing deep down what they are, not believing it to be real. Touching, she confirmed it. Black, piled high on his hand, they were the most harmless items in the world. "They're nothing. I mean, they're screws."

Romeo grinned. "Yep. Idiotic, I may be. Suicidal, not today." He took the screws and threw them gently over the rail.

Susan watched in horror, disbelief and astonishment. "What the hell are you doing?"

"Low level rioting," he grinned again. Reaching into his bag, he gently let the screws fall onto the motorway below. "The trick is not to look like you are throwing it. Everything is being watched. This is why this is such a stupid thing for me to do in the daylight. But I wanted you to know what and who I am. At least who I am now."

"This is madness. You can kill someone down there. They can blow a tyre. Crash and kill someone. Swerve out of the way, causing accidents and chaos."

"OK. Watch what is happening." He leaned over and she followed suit.

Nothing happened. The cars continued driving. Lorries, busses, cars, trucks, families, singles, playboys, perverts, good people and bad. All moved in an anonymised mass of metal that flowed ceaselessly beneath them.

"See? That's why I call it a low level riot. I am expressing myself through screws. They pick up those screws and their tyres will be flat later today or tomorrow. It will be an inconvenience. They will change the tyre with their spare and get the damaged one repaired. A few extra minutes or hours in their schedule. Nothing dramatic."

"But it could cause a blowout," Susan said. Part of her was thinking of the angles behind this madness.

"Yes. At high speed, the damaged tyre wall could give way. They shouldn't be speeding. At the posted speed, they should be safe."

"Should be? Are you now the arbiter of their lives?"

"No. The arbiter of mine. I want to be in charge of my life for once. I want to pursue what I want instead of what I should be pursuing. This is idiotic, possibly. I may be proven wrong, but I doubt it. The stakes are too high. I may be labelled an anarchist. Maybe I am just that. I want to be honest. It is what attracted me to you so strongly. Honesty in a way that hurts. That finds beauty in the kill of the lioness as well as the herd of peaceful grazers. The balance of a system must have both. Our current system is biased against the peaceful grazers in the guise of protecting them. They aren't even aware of the lionesses that are all around. I intend to open their eyes and perhaps take out the occasional lioness."

"Take out? What are you trying to be? Rambo? This is insane. If you aren't going to hurt me, please take me home now. I've had enough madness and violence in my life. I don't need more. I thought you were better than this."

"Susan. I understand. I will take you home. It was probably too soon."

"Too soon? Do you think you'll ever see me again?"

"I'm hoping." He grinned and looked straight into her.

Her entire insides went against her head. She wanted to run. Get the hell out of there. But her body yearned for the certainty of simplicity; even better, for the certainty of a complex stasis. He was that. She realised that she was holding his hand again, grabbing it when the second batch of gyproc screws went over the railing. He was next to her and not moving. Waiting for her. Willing her to move. She could feel a gravity pull her next to him.

As her body began to sway, he held her firm. "I'm sorry about tonight. All I ask is that you see me again. I'll drive you wherever you want me to take you. Victoria station? I'll drive you to your country pile if you want."

Susan wanted to say 'take me to your place', but it wouldn't come out. She wasn't ready. "Let me think about it. Walk me back to Brent Cross and I'll get a friend to pick me up."

She began to walk, her hand letting go reluctantly. The noise of the constant traffic disappeared as her mind pounded with the painful holding of contradictory thoughts at the same time. Hegelian dialectics, she muttered to herself. Fuck you, Hegel.

Chapter 22

Copycat

Romeo did not upend the rucksack. It was left on that footbridge. Someone else saw and did what Romeo was unable to do with Susan next to him. A grainy, shadow of a figure, lifting a bag and emptying its contents onto a massively busy motorway with no ransom, message, or further acts of destruction. The figure did not appear to be drunk, part of a crowd, or in any way odd. It could have been anyone. That was the main attraction to the act.

When the conservative commentators condemned the action of spreading screws on a public motorway, the reaction was opposite to that intended.

The first copycat incident occurred in Brixton, in south London. Screws were found on the A23 road outside of Brixton station. There are an incredible number of cameras in the area yet not one was able to pick up the culprits. News reporters speculated that it was expertly planned with no more than a handful of screws thrown at a time in a manner that could not be detected by the web of CCTVs that covered every approach.

Busses, lorries, ambulances, taxis and countless ordinary Londoners reported flat tyres the next day. There were no blow-outs or accidents. Just the quiet decay of some part of essential life. Air being contained in one's tyres could no longer be taken for granted.

Like pregnancies in a Secondary school, the incidents increased in scope and frequency. Two more in London, five in Birmingham, and three in Manchester. Within a week, the newspapers breathlessly reported the spread of a plague so potentially damaging to society not seen since the Bird Flu or, up until then, the radioactive poisoning of Russian spies in Salisbury. It was an unknown with no purpose apart from the attack on civilisation itself. What were they so angry about, muttered both the left and right of centre politicians. Their concern was not the banality of the screw, but future escalations. Roads and infrastructure was to be respected.

Two weeks after the nocturnal dump of screws, a reported case appeared in Moscow, Beijing, and New Orleans. Buenos Aires, Rome, and Melbourne were next. As if on cue, all major cities developed a case of the screws on motorways. There were variations. Not all were gyproc screws. Some even dumped appliances on the road, causing a number of very serious crashes with some fatalities.

It was dismissed as viral thuggery. Yet no group claimed it. No movement gave it guidance. It was a quiet discontent being aired across the countries and continents. Across ages and ethnicities.

Then, all media outlets ceased coverage of the phenomena. Instead of stopping it, people accelerated and intensified the movement. Groups began to speak out in favour of it. Greens liked that it targeted motorists as the pollution from engines were causing so much damage to the environment. Radicals liked it because it was radical, chaotic, and as close to anarchic that anyone had seen. School children would take Tik Tok videos of the individual screws that 'accidentally' fell out of their pockets as they crossed the road. Or the accidental spillage of screws in amongst the parked cars in stadiums. After the football matches, people would drive home on soon-to-be flat tyres.

The plan that Romeo had conceived with the dimpled unfired shotgun shell in his pocket was executed without him. If he turned his mind to it, he was little more than the butterfly's wing to the hurricane that was unleashed. Whether he was a cause, a contributor, or merely a participant would be determined at a later date.

For now, Romeo was in love.

Chapter 23

London (May 2019)

The new smell of Romeo's car was incongruent for Susan. The music, turned on but kept low, was tasteful and classy. The interior, immaculately clean. Not even a bug splatter on the windscreen. His aftershave or cologne, she couldn't put a finger on it, was just noticeable. Like the smell of cleanliness of a working man. You know there must be grease and sweat deep down, but he cleaned up well. It did something to her. She didn't like how much she wanted to like him. To hear him speak. To watch his lips move as he spoke. To feel his hand brush innocently against hers as he pushed a button or changed the climate control. Her eyes traced the veins that followed his thumb, crisscrossing across the back of his hand and wrist. Disappearing beneath an immaculate cuff. All while looking indifferent to his appearance.

"How are screws different from bombs?" She ejaculated.

Romeo was watching the road, now dark apart from the streetlights, headlights, and shop fronts. His movement was slow, deliberate. Hand over hand on the steering wheel, he took a tight corner before accelerating onto the motorway. He shoulder-checked, took in the mirrors and horizon, then turned to Susan momentarily. Enough to catch her eye before returning his to the road.

"You've seen Godfather III? I hated it when it first came out. The daughter was a terrible actor and it felt formulaic. However, over time, I've learned to appreciate it. One line sticks in my memory. When Don Altobello goes to Mosca, the assassin, in Sicily, he says 'I have a stone in my shoe. You can remove it.' It is a not-too subtle euphemism of someone he needs killed. Why? Because you can get used to anything except a stone in your shoe."

Susan looked at him expectantly, waiting for the connection.

"The screw in the tyre is society's equivalent of a stone in a shoe. So long as we experience flat tyres, we won't forget the message."

She looked at him a while longer. "That's it?"

"That's it. Simplicity. A form of civil disobedience aimed at property not people."

"What above the political discourse? Riots, protests?"

"The screw isn't giving a political option. It is going straight to civil disobedience and, then, …" He didn't finish.

"Revolution?"

He looked at her longer than it was safe to do so. "Yes. Why? Because political discussion has already occurred. Because people need an outlet. Like panic buying in a pandemic or hoarding generally. It is a personal manifestation of their disquiet."

Susan found herself nodding alongside Romeo. "A modern avatar. The screw."

The two sat in the silence, feeling a tension growing.

"In life," Romeo continued, "you are born into a position within society's pyramid. I believe that you need to be either on the top or invisible. Either you control the entire fucking thing or stay off the radar. I am assuming that you will not be happy in whatever position you find yourself in. If you are, great. I strive to be happy. To be content. To live in the moment and all that hippy bullshit that those without any power push as a coping mechanism."

Susan suppressed a smile. How could he reflect her deepest thoughts so completely? Was he insightful and wise or crazy and unhinged?

"Forget about your position. Let's just look at you surviving wherever you end up. Survival is about understanding the system around you and determining who is making the decisions that affect your happiness and your life. Can you do that? I sure as hell can't. And I'm considered rich. Imagine the underclasses. The 70-90 percent of the society who struggle to do their bit. Fit in. Play along. Persevere. The thing about the underclass is that one doesn't know what one doesn't know of. Unknown unknowns, to quote a famous Dick."

"And how does this lead to screws?" Susan asked, half preferring Romeo to continue his polemic.

"I'm getting there. If you wish to be the decision maker in your life, then you must be visible and have all the power or you possibly become the most powerful. The lure of becoming the most powerful is fantasy because there can be only one or handful of most powerful people. To be invisible is to be one of the millions."

"With a bag of screws that is going to make one of your underclass late for work and possibly get her fired? Or unable to take little Johnny to the hospital because her tyre is flat?" Her hair fell across her face and she brushed it away.

"Why is it always a little Johnny? Anyway, cars have spare tyres for a reason. And the purpose of this is not to hurt the little people but to empower all of us with votes. Us little people have the power if we decide to use it. I am trying to wake us up." He pressed on the brakes and merged towards the exit. "This is your exit, isn't it?"

"Uh, yes." Her voice came out softly.

"Wealth is created through a discrepancy of information or need between people. All other transactions are functional."

Susan found his voice hypnotising but not before registering that the last bit sounded a bit like Paul. She pushed herself into her chair and let his words wash over her.

"If all was known by all parties to a deal, it is difficult to see one party garnering huge wealth. Parties acknowledge a 'fair' price that factors risk of capital (intellectual capital, time capital, money capital) and extent to which the product is taken up by the market."

"Yes professor. You don't get out much, do you?" She was smiling. It felt good. A warmth spread inside her. It was nice not to be the one who pushed intellectual conversations. It was nice that he wasn't threatened by someone capable of having this conversation with him.

"I didn't know I was poor until I made my first million. I was never happy with money, but it was exciting."

"I know you've got money, maybe even rich. You know I have a few bob. No need bragging. It's not becoming." She felt annoyed with herself for telling him off, but would have been more annoyed if she didn't challenge him. If he actually thought this impressed her, it was better that he knew she wasn't that kind of girl.

"I'm trying to understand this madness of the screw myself and explain it to you at the same time. I know you're trying to derail me off this boring subject. But, to me, it is the essence of our lives. It is about power. It is what the whole LGBTQ movement is about. I believe it is the basis behind racism. So much of life's ills."

"Racism?"

"You are trying to side track me. That's hours of me babbling and I need to hear from you first. But, generally, racism is prejudice coupled with power (real or perceived). Most of it is ignorance but it is so pervasive and the power structure is such that those discriminated against have very little recourse because of the power they feel (real or imaginary) against them. Combine this with time, reinforced bigotry and ignorance, and we find an over class and underclass. The over class feels entitled to kick down on those who don't share their characteristics—one obvious being the colour of skin. But you are getting me off topic again." He reached across and put his hand softly on her shoulder as he said this. "I want to get to the heart of how we create power within society. We give it to the people we trust. We acknowledge the inequality—provided that the trust isn't misused."

Susan barely heard the last words. The warmth of his hand burned on her skin beneath her clothing. She rubbed her neck and touched the pendant that hung loosely on her chest. A reminder of Marcel. A different time. A different person. A man she felt existed only in her memory.

"And if this trust is misused long enough, it becomes a sense of entitlement. It is up to us to remind all of ourselves that we give the power and we can take the power."

"The Lord giveth and the Lord taketh away," Susan mumbled.

"We are not to suffer the abuses of power," Romeo said, happy to hear from his passenger. "We are not Job. This is not God. These are people whom we elected and whom our parents and their parents elected. It is a system engrained and in desperate need of reform."

"But you aren't talking reform, are you?" Susan said. Her head tilted down as her eyes looked up at him slightly to the side. She looked irresistible to him.

"I am, but we must be prepared for the logical next step."

"Revolution." Susan whispered the word. "Isn't that something done in history books?"

"Isn't this your place?" The motorway disappeared long ago to be replaced with A-roads and, now, B-roads and country lanes. The navigation system on the dashboard showed that they had reached their destination.

"You're a dangerous man, Romeo." She turned to look at him and didn't look at the gates as he drove through the tree-lined road that snaked through the woods before the opening presented the manor house.

"And you are a brilliant woman. Goodnight, Susan. I think I'll drop you off and not walk you to the door, if that's okay?"

Susan nodded. "Good idea. I'll see you again?"

"You'd better. I'll wait for you to call me."

The door slammed shut and he watched her skip lightly to a well-lit door in an otherwise under-lit house. She turned briefly to give a girlish wave before opening and closing the house door. He waited a moment and put the car in gear. The tyres crunched the pebble drive and he returned into the darkness of the woods and long trip home to London.

Inside, Susan felt alive. She showered and slipped in next to Paul. He felt her hands on him and responded. Her mouth kissed his. She searched her husband's body as though they were making love for the first time. Tenderly tracing his fingers, ears, kissing his eyes and face. Her body increased its desire and she began tearing at his flesh, wanting him to take her violently. She wanted to be slapped, grabbed, fucked hard. Fast. She didn't want to make love. She needed sex. She needed to get laid. To empty the tension and reset the ideas that swirled in her head. To release as many times as Paul could sustain it. To find some Viagra and feed it to him with hot chocolate and do it all again. To exhaust the thoughts that entered her head. To remind her that she was still married. Still happily married.

Chapter 24

The Derainier Estate, Sussex (May 2019)

Susan woke as Paul slipped out of bed and downstairs to make breakfast. The sheets would need changing and she needed a long bath. Perhaps a spa. What did he say? A screw? She smiled at the idiocy. If he wasn't so handsome, didn't smell so nice, didn't talk so well, she would have dismissed him out of hand. But it wasn't his looks or smell or any specific thing. It was the way he looked at her. No pushing himself. Just showing himself and waiting. To see if she responded.

She didn't want to allow her mind or body to think like this. Showering, she went downstairs to see what Paul was up to. As usual, he was too self-absorbed to understand or care about anything other than his own ambitions and which whore he'd seduce next. As if he could seduce anything.

She drove to London to meet Candace for a girl's day out.

"I hope neither of us ever have to work," Candace greeted Susan with a kiss and firm hug.

"You already work."

"I was joking. I don't know how I do it. They'll fire me one of these days."

"You want to be fired. You'll make ten times the money if you opened your own firm."

"Doctors don't make that kind of money. Not in the UK." Candace dropped her bag next to the table and made herself comfortable.

"You can always open a clinic and employ a couple dozen."

"Let's think about that over tea."

"With or without the champagne?"

"Tea without shampoo? You called me for a reason, didn't you?"

Susan smiled. "My treat, today. I need it."

"Paul being an asshole?"

"No more than usual."

"Something else?"

"Someone else."

Candace stopped fiddling with her bag and put it aside sharply and sat erect at the edge of her chair. "Now you have me interested." She exaggerated the lean-in, waiting for the gossip.

"It's the guy from the café."

"Mr. Hots?"

"He's okay."

"Have you slept with him?"

"Not yet. I mean, no." Susan blushed.

"You naughty vixen," Candace smiled as she grabbed her friend's hands. "Give me all the dirt."

"There's no dirt. He's a nice guy. Interesting."

"London's full of nice guys. And interesting. Spill it."

"He's in my head."

"And you want him in your drawers."

Susan saw the waiter come and pointed to the tea for two on the menu plus champagne and waited for him to leave before replying. "I need a friend."

"You have a friend," Candace pouted, then smiled.

"You're not a friend. You're my sister from a different universe. I love you."

Candace's left eye misted up in concern for her friend. "What's up, sweetheart? You're too sober to be so sentimental. You know I love you but you are making me concerned. Is this about a guy or you?"

"I'm my own person. It's why we get along. I don't need or want anything or anyone."

"Amen," Candace chimed in, taking a sip of the champagne approvingly.

"That's why I am struggling."

"I don't follow."

"This guy." Susan paused, turned to look at nothing in particular, and returned to take a sip of her drink. There was a further pause before she continued. "He reaches places only Marcel…" She stopped and took another drink. "I can't shake him from my mind."

Candace's hand was on Susan's and said nothing. She finished her flute and filled her friend's. As the bottle nestled into the ice with a contented slush-gurgle, she prepared to speak. "Then it's serious."

"Yep."

"Serious enough to, what?"

"That, I don't know."

"Enough to not know and to bring up Marcel?"

"He was the only man I ever loved or ever will love. That is, until now."

"Holy shit."

"Yeah. Real marital shit bliss."

"So what are you going to do?"

"Nothing. Ride it out. Ignore it. Him. Take my energies out on Paul and hope it passes."

"Paul doesn't have a clue?"

"How can he? I barely have a clue. It's something about his certainty. His clarity of purpose. His madness."

"Is he cute?"

"He's not bad looking. Smells good."

"Are we talking about a dog or man?"

"Is there a difference? But, in this case, a man. His name is Romeo."

"You gotta be kidding. You meet a man of your dreams and his name is Romeo? Top up your life insurance, sis, 'cause this is going to get rough."

"Just a name. He's a nice guy. You'll like him."

"I thought you said you were shutting him out."

"Well, I may see him again. He's got a project he's working on and he asked my opinion on it."

Candace almost spit out the cucumber sandwich she just deposited in her mouth. "Are you trying to fool me or you? You're nuts over him?"

"I don't know the guy. We just clicked. I'm married. I'm not letting this happen."

"Sometimes you don't have a choice."

"We all have a choice."

Candace dabbed the edges of her mouth with a heavy white cotton cloth. "Have I told you the story about the atom?"

Susan shook her head, mouth full of scone, cream, and strawberry jam.

"This little atom was indistinguishable from all her peers. That is, until she was split above Hiroshima."

"What the hell, Candace?" Susan said between half a laugh.

"Hear me out. We either burn long and low or fast and bright. This atom burned faster and brightest and will be remembered as long as history is written and passed on. Yet she has no name. No identity."

"Are we eating the same sandwiches and drinking the same champagne? I lost you at atom."

"I am saying that her purpose was to be. Then fates intervened and she became immortal."

"And this applies to me how?"

"You are currently existing. You stopped living when you married that bore Paul. Sorry, it's true. Now, fates have intervened and you have the chance to live again."

"And the immortality?"

"Each of us has their own fate. Destiny."

"Spoken like a woman of science."

"Hey, I'm just saying. You tell me that you met someone who has pressed something deep inside you that you thought was dead. You are existing with a cheating husband who barely knows or cares what you do. You have the chance to reignite your life. I say, do it."

"You always say that."

"Until I met Pepe. I kissed a lot of frogs before I met my prince."

"Corny. But you knew right away, didn't you?"

"I knew I was interested right away. It grew from there."

"But I'm married."

"That didn't stop Paul."

"I'm not Paul."

"Thank god for that."

The two friends drank until the subject changed. Their massage was a perfect desert. A long steam followed by tea relaxing by the pool. By the end of their day, Susan knew what she needed to do.

On the way home, slightly dozy in the back seat of the private cab, she determined not to see Romeo again.

Chapter 25

Derainier Estate, Sussex
Two Months Later… July 2019

"I've always been a corporate," Paul said between sips of his coffee. A full English breakfast filled the plate in front of him.

"And I've always been a hustler," Bob said cautiously, unsure of how things were unfolding. Paul had surprised him and he wasn't used to being surprised.

"I'm tired, Bob."

"You do look like shit, but I didn't want to say anything."

Paul grinned. Same old Robert. How could he entertain what was rumbling in the basement recesses of his mind? To do anything that might harm Bob would be unnatural; primal. Cain and Abel, primal. However, like a pimple aching to be popped, a scratch to be itched, the thought did not go away.

"You said you wanted to chat? Anything apart from the two wankers Susan is spending so much time with?"

"Feeling better?"

"Much."

"Ok, then. I know it's not good timing, but we need to accelerate matters if I'm going to be able to do my own thing."

"You know my, our, position."

"I know, I know. I can't live this life. Too stolid, too safe, for lack of a better word."

"You can visit your Marylebone club anytime you want."

"Can I bring them here? I'm just a John to them, however polite. I need to amp things up. Have networking parties. That's how you get into the big bucks. Get the boss laid in ways even he hasn't thought about. Create memories. Safe memories. He associates me with safety and fun. *Et viola!*"

Paul tried not to roll his eyes. It wasn't his style. Whoring and drugs. But it worked. Hell, their wealth was proof that it worked.

"You can't do that here. Susan may come back at any time."

Bob laughed, then suppressed it as quickly as it arose. "Paul, she's not coming back. Even if her current beau splits, I think things are over. Move on."

"I can't. I want to. You don't know what it's like. To love. To be married."

"That's why you're screwing whatshername."

"Even I don't know why I'm doing that. Boredom? Success? Expectations?"

"Loveless marriage?" Bob offered.

Paul stopped. His lips pursed. Too personal. Too close to the truth. A truth Paul wasn't happy to confront, even less to remedy.

"What do you propose, Mr. Love?" Paul tried to cover his hurt. Neither of them were fooled.

"Sorry about that. Not my place. What would I do? Start over. It also works well with my need for casholah, but that isn't the source of my advice."

"My life is one massive Gordian knot, and I'm no Alexander."

"Fuck 'em. I was feeling sorry for myself for sacrificing everything for you. For us. Now I am beginning to see that I wasn't the only one make sacrifices."

"Hardly, Bob. You've done it all. I have taken all the glory and, you, all the shit."

"Don't worry on that front. I've had lots of glory. Enough for multiple lifetimes."

Bob's face was tanned, teeth white and straight, eyes twinkling. The more likeable he was the more Paul wanted to smash his skull in. *What's happening to me?* thought Paul.

"It's all fine to say 'start over'. How? There are too many moving parts."

"Hardly," Bob said. Both his hands cupped the coffee, not unlike at Salisburys all those years ago. "It all depends on whether you mean it."

A pause hung in the air.

"You mean, whether I'm just moaning or planning. Like the difference between attempted suicide and success?"

"Yeah. You never can tell. I mean, how hard is it to kill yourself? Simplest thing in the world. Idiots with their slash marks on their wrists. Attention seekers. You want to leave, leave. If not, shut up and deal with whatever shit you need to."

Bob finished his coffee and grabbed a sourdough toast lathered in butter.

Paul exhaled as the weight of his anxiety crushed his lungs. He was in constant pain, muscles crying out for exercise or rest, he could never tell. Was he a crybaby on top of everything? Why did he find this so difficult? Who was he holding onto it for? Himself? Susan? Bob? He had no children and didn't want any. It should have been as easy as Bob said.

Chapter 26

Eight Months Later…

The United Kingdom went into lockdown on 23 March 2020. Shortly afterwards, the Prime Minister got covid and nearly died. Atlas shrugged and the world was never the same.

Susan ran away. Bob moved in, and Paul was facing a crisis in his much-loved portfolio that was beyond anyone's anticipation.

"So you are still insured against fire?" Bob asked.

"Of course. As everything is shut down, we need to occupy or monitor the spaces daily. I get photos and reports—just in case."

"In case what?"

"Our bloody building burns down. What do you think I mean? We'll lose everything."

"But you'll get it re-built."

"Yeah, but it's never the same."

"And you'll get your three years' loss of rent," Bob said pointedly.

"Yeah," Paul paused. "But everyone will be looking to do that. Insurance companies will not pay out one red penny if there is even the slightest hint of fraud."

"But you'd be better off?"

Paul thought. "Maybe. Depends how bad and how deep this goes."

"Will it wipe us out?" Bob asked, suddenly realising it wasn't theoretical.

"Hopefully not. But it'll hurt. Some of the big institutional players are teetering due to their levels of debt."

"Leverage increases both returns and risk," Bob said almost to himself.

"And markets go down as well as up," Paul replied equally deadpan. "Yeah, boilerplate 101."

"What are you going to do?"

"What can we do? Our tenants can't pay the rent so there is little we can do unless their covenant is strong."

"And we'll be judged by how we act—how any landlord acts."

"Exactly. Wartime bullshit. Reality is we have no choice. The relationship between landlord and tenant is always symbiotic. Extreme stress simply highlights this."

"You know, Paul, I think I will be going to London this afternoon after all."

"OK," Paul shrugged. "See you when I see you."

Paul leaned back and closed his eyes again. His right arm crossed his face and his forearm rested on his forehead. Without opening his eyes, he reached for the cigar.

Bob patted him on the shoulder.

The solution came to Bob as he heard Paul rail against the insurance companies and their unwillingness to pay out loss of rent or any business disruption due to Covid-19 unless the insured specifically insured against a pandemic (specific or general).

"You'll need to talk to Romeo." Bob's piercing blue eyes held the sycophant that he had been nurturing.

"You want to tag along?" The man's chin kept touching his chest. His hair was unwashed and fell over the stained shirt collar.

A wicked smile crossed Bob's face before it became thoughtful. "Sure. Why the hell not?"

Susan's eyes flashed when she saw Bob at their door. She gave the sycophant a look that made his shoulders round.

"Hi, sis," Bob leaned in and kissed her on the cheek. Her body tensed as it leaned away. She allowed the impudence more out of manners than acceptance.

"He's in the study," she said and began walking in that direction.

Romeo stood as they entered. His eyes darted to Susan as he registered Bob. She nodded imperceptibly in reply.

"I told him about the screws," the greasy haired man said to enquiring looks.

"So you bring a rapist to my home?" Romeo's voice was dangerously calm. His body squared to Bob's.

Bob, in reply, dropped his hands to his sides and inhaled deeply. He looked no more concerned than a pro basketball player about to shoot a free throw.

"Enough, both of you," Susan said. Her face was a little flushed.

The two men swivelled to look at her briefly before returning to their brewing conflict. Both Romeo and Bob stared silently at each other before the tension left Romeo's shoulders. Bob shook off the encounter, betraying nothing.

"What do you want?" he muttered at Bob.

"Nothing. I'm here to give you help."

"I don't need your help."

"Look. I don't care much about what you and Susan get up to. You want to screw each other, more power to you. You want to throw screws on the road while under some cock-a-mamey delusion that it will make any difference, that's also fine."

Romeo exhaled, glaring at his unwanted guest.

"You want to be an activist. Save the world, and all that. I have a more immediate interest in things."

"Which is?" Romeo asked.

"Not important at this stage. Suffice it to say, our interests are temporarily aligned."

Susan made to speak but stopped herself.

"You want to affect the capital structure and decision makers in power. You act under cover of darkness because you know that you are breaking the law. You hope some poor suckers will do this for you. Goring viral, I think the expression is."

Bob was in presentation mode, pitching his idea to all of them. He paced the length of the room, bisecting the space between Romeo and where Susan stood.

"Looking at successful campaigns such as Ghandi in India we can try to emulate but the circumstances are different. When dealing with an authority that has a moral compass and laws that they purport to follow, peaceful protest is best. Where there is a society run by a small number of elite then civil disobedience is best. When you have a society that is modern, robust, intricate and sophisticated, then the tools that are to be used must be anything that disrupts the smooth flow of that society.

"When we disrupt the roads and highways we stop society's smooth functionality. When we disrupt the foundation of capital, security, and risk management by attacking the insurance companies through benevolent arson, we force a rethink of how wealth is distributed and managed."

"Benevolent arson? Where is this coming from?" Romeo screwed up his face as he spoke.

"Just following on from your 'screw' premises. The ultimate objective of any social disobedience is to encourage a rethink by those in charge while providing a road plan for action to remedy the inequality being addressed."

"Forget your passive aggressive pseudo academic talk," Romeo replied. "I am proposing a quiet riot; a slow burn of discontent driven through the use of screws. You are talking about burning things."

"I am talking about impacting the real power in our society. Together, we could bring the insurance industry to its knees. Then, we have a chance to re-frame capitalism. Without a floor and ceiling, companies can't operate as we know it. Insurance is fundamental to risk management. Banks will be very different without this. Society would be very different."

"OK, but what do you hope to see achieved—apart from scores of burned out edifices?"

"Money. Justice. Recalibration." Bob's succinct use of words was a contrast to his previous verbosity.

"I'm not sure I want to ask," Romeo said. "So I won't. I think it best that you take your financial protest elsewhere. I want a movement. You want anarchy."

"No. Just what's mine. I can see I've wasted your time and mine. I won't bother you again."

With that, Bob nodded his head to Romeo and walked out. Susan followed at a distance to ensure that he left.

"Why not let it burn?" She said when she returned. "Weren't you the one who screamed 'screw you' at the top of your lungs in Hampstead Heath not so long ago?"

Romeo felt the cartridge in his waistcoat pocket. He wanted to say that meeting her had changed his perspective and priorities. Instead, "People can die too easily that way."

"And if they didn't?"

"It's just a matter of time," Romeo said, matter-of-factly.

As Susan listened, she summed up the solution: "Beneficial destruction. Not unlike economists' mantra of capitalism's creative destruction as obsolete firms die off and new ones rise from the ashes. In this case, we are part of the creative destruction."

"At what cost to us? At what benefit?" Romeo asked.

"No more than throwing a screw on the highway benefits you," she said.

"Beneficial arson?" Romeo said nothing as he sat down and held his head.

Firestarter

Two weeks later and Bob was driving by himself to one of the warehouses he described as cockroach motels ("they check in but they don't check out")—named after a pest control device sold in the US. In this case, it was a scam pretending to be a green business. Recycling tyres. Mountains of tyres inside of warehouses owned by his syndicate. One of many such warehouses owned by his syndicate. This one was near the Dartford crossing and was visible from the M25. It was one of countless others in a sprawling industrial estate servicing the key geographical location on the north shore of the Thames. Cross the bridge and a lorry driver could be in Europe in little over an hour. The other direction took a lorry driver up the M11 or along the M25 to any of the other main arteries that serviced the country. All of the major logistics companies were based there.

In the back of his Volkswagen golf were four 25 litre jerry cans. Two were full of diesel. Two were full of petrol. He had a box of long stem wooden matches for when the time came. He didn't cross the river as both the tunnel and bridge took payment using the vehicle licence plates as identifiers. He was using an abandoned blue golf's licence plates and didn't want to have to explain himself. He came up the A13 and accessed the industrial park that way. His blue golf was barely noticed amongst the hulking lorries that were in constant motion or frozen against the side of a warehouse either disgorging its goods or being stocked. He knew where he was going. It was a non-descript box of a building twice the size of a Costco in both size and height.

He parked his car where the office staff parked. He suspected that he was being watched, so he moved his car alongside the edge of the property until he saw what looked like a ridiculously small door near the rear of the building. It had no handle and looked to be made of steel. He pulled out a pack of Camels and had a smoke as he began to inspect the property. Bob brought a clipboard and hardhat to make himself invisible. If there was anything an employee hated more it was an official with a clipboard and hardhat.

It didn't take long before the door opened and a long-haired girl appeared with a guy. The girl had a cigarette already in her lips. The guy had one of those vapes. Bob politely introduced himself and calmly walked past them into the warehouse without a second look. As he passed, he could see that the two of them were more hippy than hipster. They would have fit in well in the 60s. She had hair past the middle of her back with jeans that flared at the bottom and a white top that showed her shoulders. The guy was wearing a black Metallica t-shirt and jeans that looked unwashed. He wondered if they even saw him.

Inside, there was a small room where someone had a kettle and television set up. There was a row of filing cabinets, although he had no idea what they planned to file. The administrative office was up front. Bob saw the toilet that he was looking for and went inside. He waited to hear the hippy voices pass before he opened the door and returned to the metal emergency exit. He realised that any alarms must have been turned off if they were using it for a smoke break. He stuck a piece of rubber in the door jamb to keep it open and went to the car to get two jerry cans.

Inside the warehouse proper, the smell of rubber was almost overwhelming. It should have felt hot as the weather had been unseasonably warm that summer. Instead, the air was cool and the skylights were blocked out by the mountain of tyres stacked as tightly as possible. It was clear that someone was trying to keep order. All of the tractor tyres were together. Each size of tyre was kept, roughly, with others of the same type.

There was a pile of metal where they separated the rubber from the rims. All in all, quite tidy.

Bob could hear propane-driven forklifts being operated and the voices of people doing something further to the front. There was no chance for them to see or hear him. It would have been like shouting instructions on how to operate your phone from one end of a football pitch with the recipient standing at the other end. The sound was lost, not least due to the muffling effect of the tyres. His ears felt funny. His smell was distorted. The whole place felt unhealthy and wrong.

Before Bob could back out, he opened one of the diesel jerry cans and began splashing it along the base of the tyres. He wasn't too concerned about starting multiple points as he wanted to get out fast. He emptied the diesel and left the can next to the tyres. He then began emptying the petrol. He was more careful with this as he didn't want to get any on his hands. Bob tried to remember how his father did it. Gentle splashes lapped against the already-wet tyres. He kept his feet clear. He backed towards the emergency exit, trailing petrol as he went. His hands began to shake and he put the can down. Bob looked at his hands and could smell both diesel and petrol. He felt a panic rise inside his throat.

The diesel and petrol smells were not noticeable amidst the rubber. Bob began to worry that it wouldn't light if he didn't strike the match soon. Then he remembered a story about a man who died lighting a bon fire in the country. The air was dead still and the petrol created a vapour all around him. When the man lit the petrol, he burst into flame. Bob rushed to the toilet and washed his hands, then dried thoroughly. He didn't want the match to get wet.

The matchbox was meant for lighting cigars or wood fireplaces. The wooden stem of the match was almost six inches with the delicate accelerant on the edge. He struck the side of the box and the flame came to life. He threw it on the floor and ran.

Nothing. It burned on the dry concrete until it become a wisp of smoke, catching the air currents as it rose upwards.

He took the petrol can and used it to keep the door open. He wanted to see daylight as he did this.

Next strike. Orange flame. Settled into a yellow flame. Bob turned the match around, ensuring that the wood was lit. He gently placed it next to the petrol-wet concrete. There was a soft glow that travelled quickly along the trail. It found the diesel and there was a subdued woof as the entire area burned off the petrol. It went very bright, then almost nothing. His foot was out the door and he strained to see the details. Bob refused to go until he knew it had caught fire.

The diesel ignited. It was different from the petrol. Slow. Determined. Bob saw the black smoke as the tyres began to ignite. His ears were taught in anticipation for the inevitable alarm. Or the screams from employees.

He heard nothing. He couldn't wait any longer. He closed the door and got into his car with the fake plates. His hand was almost unable to turn the ignition key. His body was in sensory overload and he struggled to swallow. He forced his breathing to slow and he put the car in gear and drove as calmly away as possible. Bob retraced his route home via the A13, never looking back apart from the occasional glance in the mirror.

Bob barely turned off the engine as he got home when his phone rang.

"You won't believe what the hell just happened," Paul's familiar voice said.

"What?" Bob answered.

"Someone torched one of the warehouses. Talk about luck! Too bad they didn't do the lot!"

"Aren't you angry?"

"Why? What a great win-win. Insurance will rebuild a new warehouse for the landlords. We don't get into any trouble as we are only in the accumulation of tyres stage, et cetera."

"No one suspects you?"

"Why would they? I'm sure the loss adjusters will need to have their say. It will be a massive pay-out. In the interim, I feel sorry for the firefighters. There must be over twenty fire trucks and hundreds of firefighters. The smoke is so bad, they had to temporarily close the M25. Can you believe that? Eight lanes cut out of traffic."

"Amazing," Bob said, trying to absorb everything. "Do they have any suspects?"

"How can they? It just started. I'm sure they'll troll the CCTV and make every effort. Some kid really pulled off a good time to go Drew Barrymore on us."

"Do you ever stop watching movies?"

"It's a classic."

"I gotta go." Bob pressed end and placed the phone carefully in his pocket. He still needed to change the licence plates back to his originals and possibly put the car out of sight for a while. Maybe best to torch the car as well. Disappear it.

His legs were sore from driving so long. Bob stretched as he got out of the car.

He washed up and went back to the Marylebone club. His smile was permanent as the hostess, wearing only a dinner jacket brought him his usual. He put his feet up and turned on the news. The blaze featured heavily across the news stations. He turned off the television and sat in the quiet for a moment. Something was changing inside him.

He liked it.

Two Months Later…Cyberspace via London (June, 2020)

"How shall I call you," Bob wrote on the encrypted service. He wasn't sure whether WhatsApp was actually encrypted or whether the security services said that so hackers and terrorists would send messages over the platform without taking the usual precautions.

"Mr. X is fine." The lines appeared on Bob's phone and he tried not to laugh.

"You were with the Extinction Rebellion? Why you'd leave?"

"You a cop?"

"No. You?"

"No." Smiley emoji. "I liked what XR were doing. The public only saw a sliver of what we talked about in our forums. We were looking to shut down entire motorways. Blow up refineries. Sink tankers. It was great stuff. What do we end up doing? Blocking streets and talking with kiddies."

"It was really effective," Bob wrote.

"Sure. But then we wimped out. There was that incident on the underground and many in the movement lost heart. They didn't want to go that route. Now the PM is talking about labelling XR a terrorist organization."

"I heard. What do you want to do?"

"Stick it to the man. Make him sit up and take notice."

"You have skills?" Bob wasn't going to spell it out.

"Yep. You have money?"

"How much?"

"What's the job?"

"I'll tell you on a more secure channel. First I need a demonstration of your willingness to impress."

"What do you want?"

"I'll leave that to you."

"Can I suggest a spot? The owner is the government of Brunei. Lots of people hate what he is doing in his own country. He has made homosexuality illegal. Punishment is death by stoning. STONING! I would like to target that place."

"In London?"

"Already had lots of press last year. Hugh Grant and countless other celebrities and wannabes picketed the spot. Lots of headline news. Do you know what happened as a result?"

"What?"

"Nothing. Not a fucking thing. It's the difference between soft and hard power. When dealing with a dictator, you need to cut off his dick. It's as simple as that. Find all his hidden dicks around the world, protected by western justice, and cut them off."

Bob began to wonder if the mysterious Mr. X was stable and whether he was going too far.

"Perhaps we should continue this conversation in a more secure place," Bob suggested.

"Don't worry. I'm not a cop. I only want justice. I'll need some dosh. I'll send you the details after this. Either you'll send the money or you don't. I'll either impress you or I won't. The rest is bullshit talk. I'll leave the rest until later. Best that you don't even know. Deniability is critical."

Bob found himself nodding in agreement as he read the blurb. He knew each of them would delete their conversation after they signed off.

"I'll send the money. You do your stuff. I'll be in touch."

"You betchya will."

Bob put his phone down and proceeded to delete all the messages. It was all too easy, he thought. The red-haired girl was a cheap closer. Paul was clueless or, at the very least, a willing sucker. How could he have made any money, he thought? He's still like a babe in the woods.

Chapter 29

One Month Later…Mayfair, London (July, 2020)

Susan and Romeo decided to celebrate with dinner at her favorite restaurant, *Le Gavroche* in Mayfair. It was the place Susan went with Candace and their friends. It was the place they planned to hold their reception when they got married. From the street, it was nothing more than a glass-paneled door with a Victorian metal and glass canopy to provide relief from the rain that more likely than not was falling on a hungry connoisseur. There was a brass plaque that sat discreetly to the left of the door. The name was spelled out simply above the door in a framed back-lit glass pane. For the uninitiated, there was nothing to draw you in.

The first impression upon entry was the color red. It was everywhere. Champagne was served as they waited to be ushered downstairs into the restaurant proper.

Young women and men filtered in alongside very refined white haired couples. First dates, with their combination of shyness and uncertain boldness. The public school boys were now politicians or business-men in the city; they still looked like they just woke up after taking a nap in their suit. The women looked im-maculate, dressed in the latest fashion. Those sporting wedding rings wore little other jewelry. Those who hadn't yet closed the deal with their partner dangled elegant necklaces, earrings, and bracelets. Romeo leaned in to kiss Susan. Her hands were in his and they were sitting so close on the couch that their hips and shoulders were touching. She radiated happiness with her dancing eyes next to Romeo.

They already knew that they were having the tasting menu, so they didn't worry about looking at the menu. It was the best choice ninety-nine times out of a hun-dred in places like this, Romeo told Susan. She already knew, but said nothing. Her hand held his and their eyes played on each other's faces.

The food was fabulous. Susan and Romeo were like a first-date couple without the hesitation. They snuck little kisses, held hands, and smiled incessantly at each other. They swirled their wines before burying their collective noses in the space above the liquid and be-low the top of the glass. They both inhaled as they sipped, allowing air in between their lips and passed the nectar into their mouths. They both smiled and nod-ded in agreement as they gave their verdicts. This happened between each of the eight courses that appeared with a delicate flourish in front of them. The cheese soufflé cooked on double cream. The marinated and glazed salmon with nuts and ginger. The seared scallop with smoked eel sauce and trout roe. The roasted John Dory glazed with shellfish sauce, cep cannelloni and cauliflower. The fregola, crispy chicken neck and skin, pumpkin and truffle. The roast venison, chickpea fritter with black garlic, parsley and red wine sauce. All followed by a selection of farmhouse cheeses, chocolate and coffee with petits fours. It was sublime and prosaic.

Anything less would have been a disappointment. Romeo reflected on the burdens of affluence on one's ability to achieve and sustain happiness. All of these experiences were wonderful and worthy of elevating one's spirits. Yet, even the extraordinary could become ordinary if you experienced it every day. By its very definition, it ceased to be extra-ordinary.

Neither Romeo nor Susan showed any sign of being less than happy. Susan's teeth flashed white as her hair fell over her shoulder and she flicked it back. Romeo nodded to the head waiter to get the bill.

"Shall we have a few more at the Dorchester?" Romeo inhaled deeply as they stepped out into the night air. His shirt was open at the neck and his navy blazer framed his torso in a way women loved. Susan looped her arm in his and put her head briefly on his shoulder.

"Sounds perfect. But I think I'll have an Irish coffee after all that. I hope someone is on the piano tonight." Susan didn't tell Romeo about the night Candace's father rescued her from the Dorchester all those years ago.

The walk didn't take more than ten minutes and the doors opened to the lobby of the Dorchester. The concierge looked up and instantly recognized either Susan or Romeo because he came over. He shook both of their hands and asked if there was anything he could do to make their stay more welcome. Romeo palmed him a £50 note and said he'd let him know.

The promenade, as the main hall was called, extended seemingly as far as the eye could see. There was no piano visible in the bar. Appropriately, it was called The Bar. It was immediately after the small shop to the left as you entered the promenade.

They were seated, given champagne cocktails (Susan forgot her earlier comment about Irish Coffee), and settled into people watching as the live music washed over them. Apparently, there was a piano.

Romeo saw the greasy-haired man who kept his chin to his chest when talking. The one who brought Bob to see Romeo the other day. He waved him over. The man looked over his shoulder to see if there was someone behind him before smiling and joining them.

After a few minutes, it became obvious to Romeo that Mr Greasy was feeling out of sorts. Perhaps it was the overly loved-up atmosphere of Romeo and Susan. Perhaps it was the feeling of being a third wheel. Greasy switched to a whiskey sour; they served him a perfect version of the cocktail. He had another. He complained that his head was beginning to feel cottony. His seat was uncomfortable, he said. It was too hot.

"I think that's it for me, guys," he said, rising carefully.

"Are you sure?" Romeo looked up at him but remained seated. His body was facing Susan. His head was strained in its turn to see Greasy.

"Absolutely. You love birds enjoy your night. It has been a great evening. Thank you both again. Next time is on me."

Susan squirmed out from her position and came over to hug him. It was gentle and sincere. She kissed him as softly as a feather on his cheek and put her hand on the side of his face. "Remember that you are loved. Be safe." He squirmed in reply and hid his blushes.

Romeo got up and shook his hand firmly and looked him in the eye. It was his trademark. He was a closer.

Greasy left, shuffling at first, then walking. The wait staff nodded as he left and one woman sitting with an older man turned to look at him as he passed.

The promenade seemed less grand when exiting. The concierge didn't remember Greasy as he slid into the outside blackness illuminated. The night was cool but warm enough for a walk. He felt like a walk. The traffic on Park Lane was subdued. Busses and taxis passed on the inside as gleaming Mercedes and Range Rovers glided by at a more urgent pace. Most days, he would not have given it a second thought. Probably private cars or playboys or diplomats being ushered between meetings or meals. Greasy began wondering how he could effectively spread screws along Park Lane and get people to slow down. Think about…

At that moment, Greasy was thrown to the ground by what felt like a strong wind. His mind saw nothing until he turned around. His hearing was different. There was a high pitch and not much else. He shook his head to make it start working again. He put his hand to his ear and felt a liquid. He looked at it on his hands. Blood. As he tried to understand what happened to his body, his eyes saw flames and broken glass where the front of the Dorchester once stood. Its famous canopy broken in pieces of stone, concrete, glass, and steel. Bentleys and Teslas were on their sides, exposing their undercarriages, tyres on fire. He didn't see any people. He only took in the big things at first. He pulled himself up and sat at the edge of the garden feature in front of the hotel and watched the flames clawing the outside of the broken windows. The scene was a picture of hell.

When Greasy finally remembered Romeo and Susan, his legs wouldn't allow him to stand up. He began to scream. No one heard him. He barely heard himself.

Chapter 30

Six Months Earlier…Williams' Family Home, Hampstead (January, 2020)

The four Williams daughters and Rose loved the intimacy of meaningless talk around the kitchen table. It was two lifetimes from her childhood, Rose mused. Today was an especially happy day as Susan gushed over Romeo and the string on her finger.

"You can get it metalized, if you love it so much. Not sure whether it can then be plated in gold but, hey, why not?" Pepe found the whole thing ridiculous and wanted to add something positive to the conversation. Candace squeezed his leg, so he knew he did good.

"Not just a pony-riding pretty face is he?" Candace kissed him before he could object to her characterization of him.

"That's clever. Thanks, Pepe." Susan and Candace backed each other up. It was an agreement they made to reverse the usual female mistake of not supporting fellow women. In this case, she really did agree.

Samantha, the eldest, stroked Susan's head like an older sister. Susan was, for the entire family, like an adopted child. They knew her for two decades. They knew Susan's highs, her lows, her reckless side, and her never-ending loyal side. Samantha's own life was full of drama, discovering the truth about herself shortly after her abortive weddings with the father of her child. As a result, Samantha neither judged nor felt the anxiety towards the future that some might have.

Elizabeth was into her third glass of wine. "What a pleasure to have a break from the kids. Sid is an angel to take them and let me have the day. I only hope that your Romeo is half as loving towards to you as my Sid."

All women and Pepe raised their glasses and drank deeply.

The doorbell rang and Rose stood with a sheepish grin. "Pizza's here." She retrieved it and placed the boxes along the granite surfaces and wooden table that filled the kitchen.

"Perfect choice, Mum," Candace said. Her hands were already breaking apart the pre-cut slices and handing them out.

Mary remained quiet, watching her sisters and mother. Her own story was buried deep inside. She preferred not to wear her heart on her sleeve or make outrageous comments. Mary's greatest desire was to write a great book, fiction or otherwise, and meet the love of her life on a book tour. They would have children and write and make love and spend all their free time with her family in this kitchen and the back garden. The Williams family BBQs were legendary. Her emotional collision with Nash was a distant memory that kept coming into focus at the most inopportune times. The way he led her on to get to Sid's money. The way she fell so hopelessly in love. The way he smelled and made her feel. She pushed those thoughts and emotions down as they threatened to dampen the happiness of the moment. She would sort herself out one day.

Jim was not there today. He was helping a local committee deal with an unscrupulous developer who was trying to open up their sacred greenbelt. He felt passionately about the survival of these green spaces within London. Rose promised to save him at least half a pepperoni pizza.

"When is the big day?" Rose asked, half-knowing the answer.

"I'd marry him yesterday if I could. Paul is being difficult."

"Do you want me to have a word?" Pepe leaned in. Candace didn't understand what he did to her, but even this made her horny. She put it down to her bio-clock and the early stages of pregnancy. At some point, she'd write about it. Right now, she was enjoying the extra kick of hormones and a willing partner to satisfy her desires. She wondered if this happened to all women. She felt sorry for men and their inability to experience this level of emotional and hormonal highs.

"No. Please, no." Susan stammered. "It'll be fine. Paul wants his pound of flesh. I'll give it to him. What do I care? It's only money."

"Spoken like someone who has forgotten what it's like to not have it," Elizabeth said.

"Pot, kettle, black?" Mary chimed in. This got a smirk and a towel was thrown playfully at her by Samantha.

"OK. Don't shoot the messenger. I'm only saying that money has a value when you don't have so much. I can't help it that Sid's family is so wealthy. It does eliminate the biggest source of arguments."

"Because you love each other?" Susan asked.

"Because he's so damn good in bed," Elizabeth giggled. "Sorry. Too much wine. He's my best friend. I knew it that first night."

"Yeah, my wedding night. How could I forget," Samantha said. She was not unhappy. It had become a point of reference for the family. Life before and life after that night over two decades earlier.

"And look how wonderful everything turned out," Rose said. Her eyes were watery from memories, both good and bad.

"Mum, when you were born, they broke the mold. You *made* it wonderful." Candace got up and hugged her mother. It made Rose cry briefly and she wiped her eyes on her sleeve.

"Stop it or we'll all set off," Susan said.

Even Pepe was silent. The distance the Williams family travelled in time, space, and enlightenment was one of the greatest attractions he had towards Candace. Compared to his dysfunctional family, the Williams were the most loving, balanced family he knew. Otherwise, there was no way they would have survived what they had gone through.

"At least we have each other." Rose said.

"And we are complying with Boris' covid rules," Mary added. "Otherwise, who knows what would befall us." Her sarcasm went unanswered …

The UK government was, like all governments, trying to cope with the virus. Lockdown. Opening up with social distancing. Less social distancing. Pubs opened. Everything opened. Then, the rules. No more than six to gather. Then, the circuit breaker shutdowns. The mental, physical and emotional strain manifesting itself in countless small ways throughout society. But all of that would happen later.

"I was thinking," Susan said, ignoring Mary, "that so many of our problems in life, in society, are down to the lack of love. Or love, unreturned. Look at us. This kitchen is like a charging center of love. I could be on my face with exhaustion and depression but this kitchen, this love, would fix me in no time. I love you guys."

"Whoa. How much has she had to drink? Let me have some of that!" Candace reached over and took Susan's glass, sniffed it, then pretended to down it in one gulp. Instead, she drank her orange juice.

Rose squeezed Susan's shoulders and said nothing. Her eyes were welling up and a lone tear fell across her cheek.

"Life is pretty good, isn't it?" Pepe added as he lifted his glass in a toast. Five boxes of pizza lay open in various stages of consumption.

Chapter 31

Mr. X

It doesn't matter how he did it. Mr. X was a man in search of significance. He tried a number of charities and activist groups, culminating in the Extinction Rebellion where he was a star until he became too radical. In Bob, Mr. X found a sympathetic ear. Bob agreed with all of X's angst and anger and need to demonstrate to the world. Bob did not judge when X talked about the need to rid the world of the virus—and he didn't mean Covid. Homo Sapiens. We were the virus that was killing the Earth, X explained. Bob nodded sagely even though they never met in person.

X relished the opportunity to show his loyalty to the cause and the importance he could bring to Bob's objectives—even though Bob didn't let him know what those objectives were. He knew he had to make a big splash. What better target than the bigoted and homophobic owner of the Dorchester? Wouldn't it be what they deserved—if each of those dictators and despots had their crown jewels obliterated and made worthless? People wouldn't feel safe staying in places where its owners were on a list of no-goodniks.

It was an easy choice. He had the skills and the means to pull it off.

The key to dismantling a modern building was to use its safety features against it. The twin towers fell because of the audacity of the plan—backed up with knowledge of demolition. The Grenfell Tower in the UK burned because the faulty cladding bypassed the containment strategy of the architects and building regulations. Mr. X's plan worked because he knew how to bypass the containment systems within the Dorchester.

X took the idea of beneficial arson and upgraded to fire and explosions. He didn't share any concern over life.

X was outraged against the Brunei's government policy towards the LGBTQ community. To think that there was state legislated death by stoning in today's world was hard to fathom. Blowing up a landmark focused minds. X was no Ghandi.

∞

As Greasy wiped the blood from his ears and glass from his hair, he called 999. After that, he ran towards the flames. He was turned back. There was nothing he could do. He called Bob to let him know about Susan. Bob could tell Paul. Greasy didn't have much to do with Paul.

When he told Bob, the phone went silent. Greasy had to say his name numerous times before he got a response.

"Susan was in the hotel?" a quiet voice asked.

"I was also in the fucking hotel," Greasy said. "Ten minutes earlier, I'd be toast."

"I, uh, I have to go. I'll get back to you. Thanks for letting me know."

Chapter 32

Dorchester Hotel, Mayfair (July, 2020)

Susan and Romeo watched their greasy friend walk away. Susan held Romeo's hand and gently kissed it before putting his hand on her cheek. The lights were low, with a glow of the red stalagmite glass around the bar. A tinkle of the piano brought them back to the present with a vocalist filling the room with a warm sound of New Orleans right there in London. Neither of them knew the large woman with the deep voice or the pianist who effortlessly created the magic and moved in rhythm to her skat.

"I have an idea," Susan whispered to Romeo as she squeezed his hand. She sat erect and began to bounce her legs, partly in synch with the music and partly out of anticipation. "Follow me."

She held him by the hand and led him out of the bar. The lights were jarring in the Promenade and they both took a moment to adjust. The closeness of the Bar was in stark contrast to this. The atmosphere. The sprinkling of people. It was a reminder of the pandemic that continued to rage quietly—the ultimate quiet riot, thought Romeo—across the capital and the world. In a moment, they began to walk the length of the high-ceilinged Promenade. The place where people around the world chose to have High Tea.

The two lovers walked deeper into the hotel. They were stopped by what looked like a waiter.

"Can I help you?" It was a genuine question. His area was almost empty and he was looking to sell some drinks or food or, at the very least, justify his employment to his superiors.

"We're just looking around, thanks." Then, as an afterthought, Susan added, "We are getting married and were wondering whether we would be able to see the Ballroom."

The waiter hesitated slightly. "It is closed but I can see what I can do. Please. Wait here. I'll be right back." He walked towards the entrance and disappeared briefly before coming back with a smile.

"Yes. I can show you. Follow me."

Susan turned her head slightly, feeling a change in the air. A decompression.

The blast that followed pushed them against one another, into the gold leafed relief that covered the wall. Immediately behind, and with an even greater force, was the debris of cutlery, glass, and plaster. Before the first second passed, a third level of material filled the air. The blast took away their ability to hear the concrete give way or the ceiling collapse. Being at the end of the Promenade, it was as though they were shot out of the mouth of a canon.

The second moment saw every cavity of the former luxury hotel fill with dust and confusion. Flames appeared, eating the oxygen, providing light to their hell.

By the third second, the alarms sounded. Those who could, scrambled from under the wreckage and escaped. The rest were fated to be consumed by the rapidly increasing fire.

Neither Romeo nor Susan nor the waiter moved.

Chapter 33

Belsize Park, London (July, 2020)

Candace received a text from the friend of Romeo. The weirdo, as she called him. All it said was that there was an accident at the Dorchester. Susan and Romeo were inside. The faint ping involuntarily called her hand to her phone just in case it was something important. She and Pepe were already in bed, lights off. As a doctor, she always answered her phone. It annoyed her when people simply ignored their phones. Why have a phone if you didn't answer it, she would say to the voice message, then hang up. She didn't bother with her number or name. They either knew her or didn't. And she never withheld her number so they could always redial.

This evening had seen Pepe and her enjoy a post lockdown feast with the family. A typical Williams BBQ, she said as she licked her fingers and downed an unacceptable amount of root beer. As she wasn't allowed alcohol anymore, she reverted to her childhood favorite drink. The entire family was present, including Sid and the children. She was rubbing her stomach, willing her baby to grow and be strong. It became the new greeting for each of her siblings as well as the nephews and nieces. They all loved Aunty Candace. Her energy filled the room and Pepe stood back and loved her all the more.

Pepe still maintained the family business of raising ponies and selling them to the rich and famous around the world. His erect carriage seemed out of place next to the care free Candace. He was and always would be an Argentinian cowboy. He accepted this. There was money in the high end sale of ponies and land management. His family managed estates for people who wanted to say they had a million acres or fifty thousand acres in Argentina. They managed the sheep, the vineyards, the offices and the industrial estates. He sat in the Royal box next to Prince Charles as they watched the polo. His family had been supplying the royal families of Europe their ponies for over five decades.

Tonight, the two were like any other exhausted married couple. Pepe's arm rested gently along Candace's thigh as she slept on her side, back to him. He loved the feel of her beneath the thin cotton top. His fingers traced her shoulders, neck and back. Her perfumed hair tickled his nose and he moved his head until his lips kissed her nape. She pretended to sleep and let out a contented sigh while wiggling her bottom against him. Too tired, he thought, as he kissed her again.

Reaching for the phone caused Pepe's head to dip into the vacant space on her pillow. He rolled onto his back, eyes tracking Candace's movements. He watched as she looked vacantly at the phone. She shook her head and rubbed her eyes, trying to see what was on the screen. She swung her legs out of bed and sat on the edge, holding the phone with both hands. Some radar in Pepe told him that this was not good.

"Everything okay, sweetheart?" He whispered.

"I don't... I'm not sure."

He sat up in bed. The cold walnut headboard felt good against his bare back.

Candace stood up and walked towards the bathroom. "I've got to go."

"Work?"

"Susan."

"What's happened? Don't tell me lover boy left her?"

"There's been an accident. Something at the Dorchester. I can't seem to get ahold of that idiot friend of his. His phone goes straight to voicemail."

"I'll take you. Let's go." He swung his legs out of bed, turned on the lights and took off his boxers, kicking them off as he picked up fresh underwear and trousers. Candace was already half dressed.

Seventeen minutes later, they reached Hyde Park but it was cordoned off. Overhead helicopters polluted the silence and emergency blue lights strobed the faces and buildings as far as they could see.

"I'm going to walk this. I've got my ID."

Before Pepe could react, Candace had closed the door and was walking swiftly towards a police officer in front of the mandatory tape that fluttered in the light wind. She pulled out her doctor's identification and had a short word with the woman in uniform. She followed the pointing finger towards the fire trucks and scrum of intense blue and red lights. It was quite a distance but she was in trainers and was already running at full speed, despite being seven months pregnant.

She approached what she assumed was the command and control cluster of people for the fire brigade. Two men were looking directly at her by the time she arrived. Her blonde candy floss hair extended behind her as her body sprinted towards the emergency crew. They were assessing whether she was a threat or a vision.

"I'm a surgeon with the Royal Free. My friends are in there and I need to see what I can do to help."

All four men were looking at her now. Their gold coloured fire kit was smudged with soot as though they were recently in the actual blaze and something fell on them. Candace knew it was all about wearing something that highlighted dirt and damage so that injuries could be minimized. The reflective strips glowed in the evening lights.

"You can't go in, Doctor. It's not safe yet."

"I'm going in or someone is going in to get my friends."

"Are you sure they are inside? Have you talked to them?"

"No." Candace had to admit.

"Are they alive?"

"I don't know," she added.

"We've got most of the survivors out," the older fireman said. Candace noticed that he had something on his lapel but couldn't make it out. "We're trying to assess the situation at present."

Candace looked around. There were at least sixteen appliances, as they called the fire trucks, stationed in a semi-circle around the fire. She assumed more were stationed out of her line of sight. Two of the helicopters were aerial appliances. At Marble Arch, where she got out of the car, the lights and chaos looked serious. That was at least a kilometer from the hotel. Up close, it was all about the power of water being sprayed and determined faces of men working as a unit to save lives and property.

"We don't know if this is a terrorist incident or just a terrible accident," continued the man. "I appreciate you coming down to help. The paramedics are over there." He pointed. "They could use a doctor. But if you can please excuse me, my men and I need to keep on top of this." He turned politely but firmly and bent over whatever plans they were pouring over when she burst amongst them. The others turned their attention away from her and joined their commanding officer.

Candace walked, legs feeling spongey after the exertion, towards the front of the hotel. The entire façade had collapsed. She pivoted and looked at the length of the hotel on Park Lane. Flames licked the walls of one of the safest buildings in London, a reputation it garnered during World War II. Each floor was either on fire or smoldering deep black smoke made alive from the disco of red and blue lights below.

What was I thinking?, Candace muttered to herself as she surveyed the carnage. She hung her credentials around her neck lanyard, walking with authority amidst the men, hoses, and machinery. She didn't feel a panic. Her body calmed itself as she did a mental triage of the bodies, broken glass, and noise. She knew she should help the medical crews, and she would, but not until after she was able to satisfy herself that she couldn't somehow get inside and look around.

The Ballroom entrance was open with hoses feeding into the space. Firemen moved without yelling or fear into the same space, disappearing into the cavernous hell. *We don't pay those guys enough*, she thought to herself as she looked up the six or so floors of the hotel and back down to the space where men and women previously dreamed of visiting in their best frocks and suits for the last century.

As she cast her eyes across the scene, one that could have been painted by a modern day Hieronymous Bosch, she realized the futility of going in. She wanted to ask the paramedics if they had a list of the injured and dead but knew only the hospitals would have that. The paper pushers would worry about that later. They were here to save lives. The dead didn't worry about when they were counted.

Dorchester Hotel, Mayfair (July, 2020)

The first consciousness was one of weight. And an odd softness with bony bits that pushed into her. And a smell that was not pleasant. More like the bin where diapers were put. It was also dark. And her mouth tasted like it was chewing on plasterboard. Her senses came to slowly. There was something other than the smell of excrement. Smoke. Her right arm was pinned and had fallen asleep. She couldn't move her fingers. Her legs felt fine. She bent her knees and pushed against whatever was on her and under her to try and stand.

The darkness was absolute. Her ears raged against a constant sound that drowned out anything less than. What? There was nothing. No external sound. Just the white noise.

She reached for the bedside light but couldn't find it. Her hand brushed against what felt like a nose and glasses. A terror clawed at her neck and upper arms. Her memory flickered and the dream continued. Was she awake?

A sickening realization washed through her as the recent events did not disappear when she opened her eyes. They were open and saw nothing. A frantic panic gripped her as she turned and explored the weight on top of her. Romeo. Surely. Then who was … ? The guy. A victim who may have saved her life. And Romeo? Did he also save her life? Would he stir?

Furniture or a door or plaster lay on top of Romeo's listless body. She began to see shapes and a source of light. Orange and warm. Welcoming.

Fire.

Shit.

A new fear, a familiar fear, triggered a strength within her. She was calm. She needed to remain calm. Get out from under Romeo. Find help. Everything would be okay.

The light grew in size, giving perspective to the room she was in. It was the ballroom. The chandeliers remained fixed to the ceiling but parts of the ceiling were hanging precariously and without pattern to her untrained eye. The walls were unable to resist the flame's attraction. The air became visible, full of dust and debris.

The man beneath her looked dead. His head was twisted unnaturally. She pulled on Romeo's body, to turn him over. To see him. To kiss him one last time, if need be.

His hands, delicately caressing her beneath the duvet, lay lifeless beside his body. She became aware of her own breathing. The dust would kill him if she didn't wake him up.

"Please be alive," she prayed to herself and any God that would listen.

Susan brushed his hair and face, searching for a twitch or movement. She traced his lips, then opened his mouth and put hers to his. Exhaling while pinching his nose. Pushing on his chest. She needed to inspire him, as God did Adam, with her breath. Again. Pushing. Again. Pushing. Praying. Again. Pushing.

Romeo convulsed and rolled instinctively to his side. Susan left her hands on him to guide and feel the life restart in her lover. She could not see the tears mingle with the dust on her cheeks.

"Where..?"

"Shh. Something's happened. We need to get out."

"Are you okay?"

"I'm fine. That guy's not." She pointed to the Promenade's top waiter. "I checked his pulse. Nothing. I think his neck is broken. I think he saved our lives."

"And you saved mine." His voice was weak. Romeo tried to stand up but was forced to rest on his knee and extended arm.

"Let's get out of here. The fire is getting closer." She could feel the warmth and crackle of the orange beast. It was stalking them. Patient, with absolute determination.

She put his arm around her shoulder and heaved him to his feet. Once standing, he paused briefly, and was able to continue on his own. They walked towards the direction of the Park Lane exit but were forced back into the room that once fit a thousand political donors. Or a ball for a young Princess Elizabeth, the day before she announced her engagement to Phillip Mountbatton. Ghosts of Elizabeth Taylor and rocks stars and billionaire playboys cried as their indestructible playground burned on all sides.

"There's no exit," Romeo said, whirling around. Fire or impassible doors blocked every way out.

"There's always a way," Susan said, also looking in every direction.

"It's these fucking mirrors. I can't see where the hell the fire exits are. They must be right in front of our noses."

"There!" Susan grabbed his hand and started running towards burning curtains.

As they approached, the exit became clear and Romeo hit the doors with all his weight, half expecting them to be locked.

The two tumbled outside, picked themselves up, and continued running until they got to what looked like a service access. Romeo's hand was slippery inside Susan's as they ran to Deanery Street. Instead of turning back to Park Lane, they slowed to a walk.

"You're bleeding," Susan gasped as she looked at her own hand, then his. *Her Marcel*, her mind whispered. She could see blood dripping off his fingertips. His eyes stared at the oncoming traffic, looking for something.

"We need a cab. We need to get to a hospital."

Susan didn't argue. She was glad to be alive. She could hear the distant sound of sirens, or maybe that was her tinnitus. She had been relieved when Romeo began breathing and her ears allowed her to hear him.

The streets were quiet. They were the only people on the street. A car with a noisy muffler and glowing lights on its undercarriage drove by at speed. A sedate Volvo turned onto their street and glided by. No cabs. Susan wondered whether she should stop the next car.

The sirens became increasingly loud. Susan wondered whether they should turn back to Park Lane as that is where the emergency vehicles would target. She pulled on Romeo's hand and changed direction.

"We have to go back. There's nothing here." She was yelling, unsure of the correct volume to get through to him.

Romeo stopped but did not turn back. His body leaned forwards as if into a strong wind. His face was waxy white. After about ten seconds of resistance to Susan's plan, his body collapsed on the pavement.

Chapter 35

Candace

Pepe was moved on by police trying to divert traffic and set up a suitable cordon around what was quickly becoming an international incident. He made his way to Grosvenor Square and texted Candace to meet him there. It was the former home of the American embassy. He half expected it to be cordoned off due to the number of high value diplomats and officials who lived in and around the area. It was open. He pulled into a vacant parking bay, a rare find during the day and a thankful reprieve for that evening. He put on the radio and closed his eyes. He knew it could be a while.

Three loud knocks on the passenger window accompanied by frantic sounds of the door handle being opened unsuccessfully woke Pepe from what he hoped was going to be a good nap. He saw the blonde hair, then lips and eyes of his wife. He still couldn't believe that she married him and that they were going to have a child together. He unlocked the door and she quickly got in.

"I can't find Susan," she said. Her hair was wild from running, sweat, and soot. Pepe thought she never looked lovelier.

"Hospitals?"

"Lines are jammed. Almost no way of finding out apart from visiting each one." Her voice betrayed a frustration as much as rejection of not having found her friend.

"Then I guess we start with one and go from there." Pepe put the car in reverse and began driving north. "Which way?" he asked as he made his way through the subdued streets. Just a couple of hundred yards from the Dorchester Hotel and it was as though nothing had happened. *Keep calm and carry on*, he thought as he drove.

"There are quite a few to choose from. St. Thomas Hospital is south of the river. It is excellent. But I think they'll be taken to either Imperial College in Paddington or University College in Westmoreland or University College London. I can't imagine them going all the way to the Royal Free where we are." She was silent, unable to make up her mind.

"I don't know which way to go, Candace. You have to make a decision."

"Let's go to University College Westmoreland. I don't want us to chance the traffic on Edgeware Road. It'll be a nightmare to cross. We can then try UCL and then either double back to St. Thomas' or go for Royal Free."

"Won't the hospitals know between themselves who has admitted whom?"

"I don't know. I've never been in this situation before. I tend to get paged and then patch up the people. Mostly drunks and RTAs in the evenings. They will have declared a major incident and a protocol will kick in. I'm surprised I haven't been paged."

"Day off, remember?"

"In emergencies, doctors don't have days off." Candace's jaw was set. She had seen enough of life and death in the operating theatres. There was no room for sentimentality. Some of her patients were little more than pieces of meat that she had to declare dead. Others looked heathy enough and slipped away like sand between her fingers. She tried to be stoical but it was the worst part of her job. The job that wasn't a job. Nothing could be a job if you loved it and she loved what she did.

Pepe drove through the streets, listening to the radio for updates. Nothing apart from presenters saying that a major incident had taken place and to avoid the area. It was the same after the July 7th bombing. The broadcasters must have had a protocol in place to placate the public. Somber music was placed on the classical stations, rock stations played music that wasn't angry.

Anything to keep the public from rising up and articulating their anger or fear in the form of crowds.

They got to University College and Candace burst out of the car. Pepe idled the engine and waited. When he was moved on, he circled and returned to the same place. Twenty minutes later, Candace returned. She was flush with frustration. Due to the covid restrictions, it wasn't possible to enter the hospital or to ask questions. It took all of her persuasive powers to learn that neither Susan nor Romeo were there.

"UCL, Peps. Up to Marylebone Road and hang a right."

"I know UCL. Samantha gave birth there shortly after we met, remember?"

Candace's face softened and her hand went to his face. She remembered her father, Jim, crying as they entered the hospital when he heard that her sister, Samantha, was going to have a little girl and Pepe reassuring him that real men cried. He was not afraid to step in front of danger and fight for her. He was not afraid to let his tears flow when he was emotionally touched by an event or moment. He was not afraid now, when she needed him to be a rock.

They sped to the next hospital. Candace burst out, again, and did her best to locate Susan. This time she met a sympathetic man in a high visibility vest at the ambulance entrance. He remembered two people who fit their description because of how they had arrived. Instead of going to A&E, they presented themselves where the ambulances disgorged their contents. The two of them looked as though they had come from a horror movie casting. Covered in grey ash, streaked in water and what looked to be blood. She was able to walk. He was being helped by the woman and another person who drove the car to the ambulance bay.

Candace's heart sunk and leapt in a convulsion of dread and hope. Dread, that they had gone through such an ordeal. Hope, that they were still alive. She called Pepe to tell him the news and that she needed to find a way into the hospital, protocol be damned. He smiled through the phone and said he would wait for her on the side streets and to let him know how it went.

With her NHS credentials hanging from her lanyard, she marched in with the next pair of paramedics who wheeled in a patient on a gurney. The patient looked like a young woman, mid-20s, who had either passed out from drink or drugs. No friends accompanied her. Most likely her stomach would be pumped out and she would be given fluids to recover. Candace was disgusted at the waste of NHS resources by irresponsible kids until she remembered that she had been young and extremely irresponsible in her day. It could have been her on the gurney. Hell, it had been her on a gurney more than once.

Ensuring that her doppelganger was in safe hands, she did her best to walk her doctor-walk which ensured that no one asked her any questions as she breezed through ward after ward in her search for Susan.

When she spotted Susan, she had to stop in order to gather her emotions. Her friend was covered with a grey dust reminiscent of 9/11 survivors. Streaks of blood and something else covered her back. Her dress was hanging on by threads. Candace composed herself and took off her green bomber jacket, walking at speed to Susan.

"Thank God you're alive!" was all she could imagine before the two embraced. The nurse looked away as the swell of raw emotion overtook her briefly. The two friends held each other tight. Susan didn't feel amazement or any emotion apart from certainty that Candace would be there.

"I'm sorry I didn't call," Susan began. As she registered what she was about to say, she broke into a mad grin that summed up her frustration, terror, and love of the moment. Lines crossed the remaining grey dust on her cheeks.

Candace noticed Romeo for the first time. He was being attended to by a nurse. Cleaning his skin to take bloods and attaching the monitoring service. The doctor would attend shortly. Candace was not prepared to wait. She asked the nurse the status of the patient, instructed her to begin an IV of fluids while they waited for the test results. She did a cursory examination of the body. Breathing, fine. Pulse, weak but not alarmingly so. Blood oozed from his abdomen and she knew he needed to go to theatre. She couldn't operate on him even if he was in the Royal Free and under her. She instructed the nurse to prioritise Romeo and get him prepped for surgery. The bleeding needed to be staunched or he would die. Triage was the same everywhere.

Susan watched, knowing that the bleeding would have been noticed by paramedics if they had come by ambulance. As it was, they managed to flag down a kind stranger who had no qualms about blood on his car seat. He took them straight to UCL as it was the only one he was familiar with. As Candace found out, they snuck in via the ambulance bay and were seen to by nurses. Candace had arrived before any doctor had been able to assess Romeo. Her biggest fear was that he had slipped into unconsciousness. She had no idea of how bad the bleeding was or what was damaged. Susan felt it was all her fault. If Romeo died, she wasn't sure whether she could continue. Not again. She couldn't lose two soulmates in one lifetime.

"Have you eaten?" Candace's voice was calm, searching. Her arm was around Susan.

"Dinner, of course. And some drinks. Well, quite a few drinks."

"Wait here while I get you a snickers or whatever sugary crap the vending machine in the waiting area has. You need to start taking care of yourself. When I get back, we'll get you cleaned up. And, here, make sure you wear my jacket." She picked up the jacket she took off earlier and put it around Susan's shoulders.

Susan nodded and sat down where Romeo lay.

By the time Candace returned, Romeo had been taken to theatre and the ward matron was aware of Susan. They were informed of the explosion and had a stream of injured coming in from the Dorchester. All of the other hospitals shared the burden. She handed Susan two snickers and a pack of salt and vinegar crisps.

The two sat in silence, their conversation unspoken. Unnecessary. Candace was glad Susan was alive and relatively well. At least on the outside. Inside, she had more cuts that would scar. More pain that would need healing. Time that she may not have.

When Susan finished eating, Candace took her by the hand and led her to the toilet. Inside, she washed her face and sponged as much of the dust off as possible. They shook her hair and contemplated running water through her hair but decided against it. Being in a hospital in a pandemic was bad enough. Wet hair was a step too far.

Susan wouldn't leave Romeo until she knew what was happening with him. Candace tried to coax her to leave and return in a couple of hours.

"With his injuries, it will be at least a couple of hours before we can see him," Candace said. Her arm was around Susan. They sat next to each other in two separate chairs, still next to the bed Romeo had been lying in moments earlier. She knew that they would soon be shooed out to the waiting area to take in another patient.

"With his injuries, Candy, I may only have a couple of hours left with …," her voice caught before adding, "him." Susan bit both her top and lower lip, causing her eyebrows to furrow.

Candace nodded and they sat a while longer before being moved to the waiting area.

It was 1.03am. It was unlikely that they would see Romeo until later that morning. Even if he was in theatre at that moment, he would need to be moved to a recovery room and then, if stable, to a bed where Susan could see him. Candace called Pepe and told him to go home. She'd call him when she knew more. Most likely around noon. Susan looked up sharply in surprise at her friend's estimate of time to Pepe.

The two talked. There were no magazines due to the pandemic. They weren't supposed to be waiting either but Candace's NHS credentials allowed them to bend the rules a bit. There were so many stories of family members dying without their husband or wife or loved ones. She was thankful that there was some relaxation of the rules for her and Susan.

Exhaustion and the collapse of adrenaline in Susan eventually saw her fall asleep against the shoulder of

Candace. After a period of timelessness, Candace drifted asleep.

They were awoken to a police officer who was saying something in front of them. It took a while to understand him. Candace glanced a look outside. Dawn was giving definition to the buildings and cars outside. Inside, the hospital was quiet; reverent, as though unsure of what was happening next. Everyone was clad with masks, some with visors and masks. Most with plastic that covered their scrubs.

"Are either of you Susan Derainier?" The officer asked. He stood the requisite two metres away and wore a mask. His voice was muffled. He was forced to repeat the question three times before Candace's unconscious dragged her back into conscious interaction with the world.

Her eyes were still closed as her ears registered the question. She tried to blink but the sandman had firmly sealed her eyelashes. She dreaded to touch her eyes, the number one rule in avoiding contagion. She forced her eyes open, sensing the scratchy crystals that would dissolve and be wiped out after she squeezed some Purell on her hands.

"Is there something wrong, officer?" Her eyes batted in an attempt to see clearly. A film persisted despite her best efforts. As she moved, Susan woke and inhaled deeply and slowly as she registered where she was.

"Are you Mrs. Derainier?" He asked Candace.

"No. I am," answered Susan, suddenly wide awake. "What's happened?"

"Nothing ma'am. I need to ask you something in private."

"You can speak freely. This is my sister," Susan said, clasping Candace's hand as she said it.

"OK. There's been an incident and we need to talk to you at the station. Do you think you can do that?" He only now seemed to register that Susan had been in some trouble herself. The green bomber jacket covered up the tattered evening dress and scratches, now bandaged. Her face was clean but her hair looked out of place with the woman, he thought. She was too beautiful and worldly to appear in public with her hair matted. "You don't mind me asking, but were you involved in the Dorchester bombing?"

As he said the words, Susan felt a tidal wave of emotion crash within her. Hot, cold, dread, exhaustion, terror. Everything made sense with the official utterance of that one word. Bomb. No accident. It could never have been. Everything she had done. With and without Romeo. Because of Romeo. Despite him. All of the consequences stood in this avatar in front of her. A figure that was insignificant as he was probably a new recruit, fresh out of the academy. But he was part of the unblinking eye. The security that protected against fear and terror. The people who stood between the law-abiding public and the hordes of deceivers and thieves, burglars and murderers, terrorists and war. Her flirtation with screws and the rest made her nervous.

"Uh, yes, sir. I was inside with my fiancé when it all went… uh, black. I'm okay. My fiancé is in theatre, or, out. Not sure. I'm just waiting to find out."

"We won't be long, I'm told." His voice was soft, caring. He couldn't have been more than twenty-five years old. If he registered the incongruence between Susan the married woman and her reference to her fiancé, he didn't show it.

"Does she have to go, officer?" Candace asked. She could feel the tremors against her body from Susan.

"Of course not. But it would assist us."

Susan had grown up respecting the police. Authority. Her parents. The institution of marriage. It was why she had not yet divorced Paul. Her first reaction was to obey. To meekly follow the officer and see what life had in store for her. She remembered overhearing conversations that Romeo had with his solicitor. *Never say a thing. Let them do the talking and call me as soon as you can. I'll sort everything out.* The words echoed in her head. Should she call Peter? She needed a solicitor. Maybe. Maybe it was nothing. She'd call Peter if things changed.

"OK. When?"

"Now, if you are able."

Susan shot a look at Candace. "You'll stay?"

"I'll be here when you get back and when Romeo opens his eyes. You go."

Susan hugged her friend and stood up. Candace also stood, somehow feeling it awkward to be the only person sitting. She watched Susan follow the officer out the secure doors and out of sight. The digital clock on the wall showed 7.29am

After a moment of contemplation, trying to understand what just happened, Candace approached the nurses station, hoping for an update on Romeo. She could see the strain on the faces of those who hadn't yet changed shifts. The bomb added pressure to an already over-stretched hospital.

"Are you family?" the smiling face asked?

"Yes," lied Candace.

The nurse poked on her computer and consulted one of her colleagues. Her skin was flawless with teeth and eyes that hypnotised Candace. In any other setting, she would have commented on the striking appearance of the nurse. Her colleague, on the other hand had pock-marked skin from either excessive acne or some other dermatological nightmare as a teen. She kept a passive face as the two looked increasingly professional. She knew from experience that wasn't a good sign.

"The good news is that his operation was a success. The doctor will be able to come out and brief you momentarily. But he will need some rest. The best you can do is either go home or sit where you were and we'll come and get you." The nurse didn't understand why Candace was able to flout covid regulations and she wasn't going to ask. She did know that both Candace and Susan were not posing a problem and she wasn't going to become a problem unless they forced her to.

"Thanks. I'll carry on waiting."

Four hours passed and Candace called Pepe to update him on the situation. There was little either of them could do. If she hadn't promised Susan, she would have gone home and waited for a phone call.

Shortly after a lunch of crisps and a terrible coffee, Susan appeared. Candace tried to leap up but her legs were stiff from the stationary morning and insufficient sleep.

"How is he?" Susan asked in a hushed tone as she sat down next to Candace. "I brought some lunch but they wouldn't let me past the door with it. I had to chuck it." She said nodding apologetically to Candace's pathetic lunch.

"Don't worry about lunch. I'm not that hungry. Romeo's fine. Operation went well. Doctor came out and confirmed and said we just have to wait for him to wake up. Should be anytime now."

Susan's mouth tightened wistfully. "Then everything will be okay?"

"Looks like it. Maybe you should get a lottery ticket when we go home. Considering what the two of you've been through…"

"I'll take my Romeo. No more chances for me for a long time." Susan was nodding from her waist with her eyes closed, hands on her lap, knees tight together.

"Oh, what did the police want?" Candace had almost forgotten why she had been waiting alone.

Susan shrugged her shoulders. "Still not sure."

"Nothing?"

"They wanted to take a statement about the bombing. No big deal."

"You would have thought that it could have waited until you got home and changed. You're traumatised. What could you tell them today that they couldn't have waited until tomorrow?"

"I was too tired to argue with them, frankly."

Candace didn't take any further notice as the two of them settled into their chairs and waited to see Romeo.

Chapter 36

Romeo

It was good to breathe the outside air. Kicking the doors open took more effort than finding the last three miles in the marathon he was foolish enough to enter fifteen years earlier. Knowing Susan was safe was all that kept him going.

A pain he had never felt before grew from a tickle to a clawing that he pushed down in his need to get safe. Stumbling onto the street, a lifetime distant from the other side of the hotel where they should have gone. One car, then another.

Then, black.

He could feel Susan and another man grabbing at his arms to try and drag him from a car. He did his best to walk. To assist. The white lights bathed him as he tried to make out colours. Yellow. Blue. Red. Talking. He wanted to thank the person but he couldn't focus.

Then, black.

He was lying on his back. Susan was crying. He could feel the sobs more than hear her. She was shouting to get some help. A person, nurse likely, began to touch his arm.

Then, black.

He woke as if everything he had experienced over the last two years was a dream. It caused a panic. His body jolted in surprise, seeking out the familiar bedroom windows with the Hampstead green that filled every vista. Instead, white ceilings, white walls, and pale blue paper curtains filled his view. He moved his arms and legs. No pain. He tried to roll over on his side and felt a searing white pain that was bearable only with the dulling opiates that coursed through his body. He realised that he was in a hospital. He was in an accident. He must have had an operation.

Where was Susan?

He called out and a nurse appeared. She smiled at his energy. That was a good sign, she said. She did a quick look at his vitals and said she would find his fiancé.

Twenty minutes, an hour, five minutes, Susan came through the curtains with her friend, Candace. Susan was flush, holding back any emotions that he knew would be triggered with the slightest comment. He became concerned when he saw Candace's face. She was deadly serious, albeit with a smile that he feared was more professional than real.

"That bad, eh?" Romeo said, trying to smile. His blue eyes bore like lasers out of his head into Susan and, then, Candace.

"You're alive. That's all that matters," Susan said. She held his hand, afraid to hug him.

"It'll take more than a building collapsing on me to slow me down," he said with a bravado he didn't feel.

"I'm pleased that you're feeling ok, Romeo," Candace said. "You gave us all a scare."

"Are you going to fill me in? I'm a bit in the dark," he replied, all bravado gone.

"You lost a lot of blood. You had some organ failure. The surgeons got it in time. You'll need to have some more surgery, but you'll be fine." Candace was not giving him all of the details at this time.

"Are you saying I am missing some body parts or will be?" Romeo said, smile returning.

Susan couldn't hold back the tears any longer. "I'm sorry, sweetheart. I told myself that I wouldn't cry."

His mood changed. He forgot about himself and rubbed Susan's hand as she held his. "That's ok. We can talk about the details later. Bottom line, am I going to live?"

There was a hesitation as Susan looked backwards at Candace. "Yes. Unless something really odd comes out of the woodwork, you'll live," Candace said.

"You'll need to make some changes to your lifestyle going forward."

"Done," Romeo said, as though negotiating a deal.

"Candy's serious," Susan said. "We'll need to make some serious decisions."

Romeo felt a shock run to his legs. He thought he had moved his arms and legs earlier. Was he imagining that, too?

"Will I be able to walk? Am I going to be able to take care of myself without a helper?" Romeo had sworn that he would kill himself before he became one of those.

"Yes, my love. You'll be able to walk, maybe even dance. We'll learn more as the days go by. All indications are positive. The most important thing is that we have each other."

Romeo reached for Susan and she leaned in to kiss him gently. Candace had her hand briefly on Susan's back for support. She still hadn't heard what happened to Susan when she went to the police station.

"I guess I am the luckiest guy in the world," Romeo said, tears threatening to fall.

"We both are," Susan said. Her eyes were closed.

Susan

The police officer who took Susan from the hospital to Charing Cross police station indulged his guest and lit up the lights. The car wasn't powerful but it was a new model and was able to accelerate and brake as much as city traffic allowed. Seated in the front seat, she enjoyed the alertness of traffic to the strobing lights and, on occasion, the siren when going through red lights or stationary traffic. The savannah cleared to allow the top predator through. She looked at the driver but he did not betray any enjoyment. Concentration or power trip, she thought.

The actual police station, from the outside, was quite pleasant. Painted in a fleshy yellow cum magnolia, it fit in with the affluence of the surrounding buildings. Across the street on the corner was Brigit's Bakery. She didn't take time to see if they served doughnuts. The idea made her a bit giddy.

Prior to leaving the hospital, she did her best to clean herself up. Her hair was still caked with dust of indeterminate origins. Her face was devoid of makeup after being scrubbed with liquid soap and hot water. She had taken off her dress to wash herself the best she could. It felt doubly dirty when she put it back on. Her clean skin registered the dried blood, minor tears, and the way it didn't sit right on her anymore. Her nose registered the stench of smoke infused in the material. It felt and smelled like clothes that hadn't been cleaned yet still worn for over a month in a construction site. The only consolation was the green bomber jacket that Candace gave her.

The officer waited patiently as she made her way from the police car to the front of the building. Four Doric columns with two Victorian styled lanterns on posts stood sentry. The officer gave her his name but she couldn't remember it. He took her straight through to Constable Norrischuk. Or, more correctly, she was taken to a small interview room and told to wait. Norrischuk joined her shortly afterwards.

"How are you doing? Susan, is it? I'm Constable Norrischuk. You were inside when the bomb went off, weren't you?"

"Uh, yes."

"And you were at the hospital? They discharged you?"

"Well, I was told to come. I'm not sure if I'm discharged or if I can go back. My fiancé is there in critical condition. He's in theatre as we speak. I wouldn't have come, but I was told it was important."

"Do you have any idea why you are here?" Norrischuk had pulled out a notepad and was ready to talk.

"I was going to ask you the same thing." Susan's voice was glad it had some small talk before she had to think and speak. "Am I in some type of trouble?"

"Oh, no. Hardly," Norrischuk said. "Although you being here is definitely out of the ordinary."

Susan's natural suspicions made her look at the door. Wondered whether it was locked. Whether they were being recorded. Who was this woman who was questioning her. "May I ask why I am here if you are not going to interview me?"

"We have a person of interest who has asked to talk to you in person. He was rather insistent."

"How do I know him?" Susan asked, feeling increasingly uncomfortable.

"Apparently, he is a friend of your fiancé?" Norrischuk looked up from her notebook to see Susan's reaction.

Susan betrayed nothing. "OK. I still don't know what this could be about. But if it will help you catch the people behind this, I am more than happy to help."

"Right-e-oh," Norrischuk said and stood. "Follow me."

The door was held open for Susan but she indicated that Norrischuk go first if only for the reason she knew where she was going.

They walked down a corridor and through a security door that required a swipe of a card followed by a lock that needed buttons pushed before they could proceed. Third door on the left was the destination. Norrischuk stopped and motioned with her head that this was the place.

"You can leave at any time by calling to a guard. I will post one outside of the door. They won't be able to hear you talking, but they will hear a holler. You ready?"

Susan nodded and Norrischuk opened the door and walked in with purpose. Susan could see that this was a practiced entry. She noticed the coat rack in the corner and the four chairs. At the table was Romeo's friend. *The weirdo*, as Candace called him.

Scapegoat

The door closed and the two looked at each other for a moment before Susan spoke.

"What's this about?"

"I wanted to see you before I went inside."

"What do you mean?" Susan said, genuinely confused. They were both seated, one on each side of the table. She sat where Norrischuk had sat. Now, it was just the two of them.

"I confessed to most of it. The screws, the fires. I'll confess to the bomb as well if need be. I know that neither Paul nor Bob had anything to do with it but I want you to get their money." He had a sheen of perspiration on his forehead and his eyes were wide open. He sat forward in his chair, elbows on the table with hands close to Susan's. If Norrischuk had seen him, she would have been shocked that he had that amount of emotion in him. During his entire conversation with her, he remained calm and matter-of-fact.

Susan's head pushed back as she sat up straighter. Her mind was racing, trying to understand the twists of the last few hours. As she didn't say anything, he continued in a voice just above a whisper.

"I know you did it. All of it. The screws at Brent Cross, the fires near Dartford Crossing, and the bomb at the Dorchester. In the last instance, the timing was inconvenient. You didn't factor in almost dying."

A cold shot down Susan's leg and her stomach shrunk. The room moved five degrees then righted itself.

"I think you're delusional, man. You've spent too much time with Bob. Perhaps smoked something?"

"I know, Susan. Don't worry. I'm not saying anything. I've decided."

"I don't understand," Susan said, still shaking her head. "You're coming across a bit crazy, you know?"

The man on the other side of the table ignored her and continued. "In biblical times, the chief rabbi took two young goats. One, he sacrificed. He said prayers over the other, and released it into the wild to carry away the sins of the community. The one released was the scapegoat."

He looked expectantly at Susan, still sitting at the edge of his seat, eyes wide and searching her face.

"Then, I am *your* scapegoat," Susan said with a wonderment she didn't feel until that moment. "For you are being sacrificed and I am being set free." She wanted to run, to bang on the door for the police officer. But she was also shaken to see Mr Greasy talking like this. He was at the restaurant; at the hotel when it blew.

His face relaxed when he saw her comprehension. "So you are." The sense of being connected warmed him.

The two sat in silence as she took in the enormity of what he was doing. Not just offering. Not threatening. Doing.

Did.

"Why?" Susan asked. "Aren't you married? What was all that I heard from Romeo about you and that girl or girls who broke your heart?"

"I'm not married. Was never married. Will never marry." His voice was calm. It felt rehearsed. "I wanted to marry but only for love. Thus far, my relationships have crushed me. I gave and got nothing. There have only been three women I have ever loved."

Susan asked the obvious.

He paused, this time a little uncertain. "My first love was Reena. I never kissed her and managed to fuck up a hug. I spent the rest of my life regretting that I didn't pursue her."

Susan had too many questions so she remained quiet. She could see that he was struggling with his response.

"My second love was Irma. Her name was the only thing old fashioned about her. She gave me what I wanted at the time but not what I needed. She nearly broke me."

Susan tried to hide her shrug. She had spent a lot of time with him over the last few months with Romeo, but she had to concur with Candace's assessment of him: weirdo. She watched him continue the conversation in his head. It was clear that a lot was going on between his ears but he didn't include her. Eventually, she asked her final question.

"Who was the other one?"

He looked at her, slightly startled from his internal dialogue. He spread his hands on the table and brushed off invisible dust before wiping his palms on his legs. He glanced at the coat rack that continued to baffle him, then each of the walls. Finally, he set his eyes squarely on her.

"You."

Chapter 39

Part Three—Susan

Susan clawed at her neck, gasping for air. The feeling of the scratchy rope both tickled and strangled. Red spots filled her blackened vision. Her shoulders ached against the unnatural angle in which they were forced to remain. Her chin lunged forward and mouth opened but nothing came out. Her body tensed and readied itself for death.

"Susan," a voice said. Softly at first, then a little more urgent. "Susan, it's OK."

She felt a palm of someone on her face. It was wet against her tears. She opened her eyes to the harsh glare of fluorescent light and the smell of disinfectant. Two blue eyes stared at her, framed by candy floss blonde hair. Candace was saying something but Susan couldn't hear it.

"You're safe. You're in a hospital. Everything is OK."

Candace's words covered Susan like the smooth waters in a gentle stream washed over ancient rocks. Susan exhaled and rested her head on her friend's shoulder. They were all alone in the hospital's seating area; no visitors were allowed. Romeo was in post-op recovering from what the doctor said was a successful procedure.

"I'm sorry," Susan whispered. She let her entire weight lean against her friend. Candace said nothing apart from her hands which stroked Susan's face and rubbed her back.

"It was just a dream," Candace whispered. "Just a nightmare. You are OK."

Susan lifted her head, skin blotchy from the heat and tears next to Candace's neck. She adjusted her hair that lay matted against her face around the back of her ears. Her breathing was deep and determined. Then, slowing, and shallow. She looked around and saw the empty chairs, the lone sentinel nurse behind her station, and the sunlight streaming through the windows to the world outside. She felt the soft touch of Candace's skin against her face, arms, and back. When she was able to raise her eyes to meet her friend's, she saw a smile through bleary eyes.

"I'm okay," Susan said. "Just a bad dream. I get those from time to time."

"I know, remember?" Candace wasn't sure that her friend was fully back from wherever she had gone in her sleep.

Susan shook her head, determined to return to the present. Fearful of the doors that led her to the past. The doors that opened when she closed her eyes. Where time was irrelevant and hurt never healed.

She stood up carefully and walked a few steps. Her shirt was wet and she looked in vain for her wardrobe. She reminded herself that she wasn't home. She looked at her hands and a new memory crashed into her. Dried blood. Remains of soot that the foamed soap couldn't remove. She looked at Candace and saw a gaunt face that tried to smile, to hide the worry and exhaustion. Candace's lanyard was tucked neatly into an unseen pocket. Her baby not yet visible. The present came into focus and the room shifted briefly. She was back. They were memories. She felt her neck. Her hands were free. No rope. No Marcel.

Her shoulders dropped slightly at the realization. The attack. The rescue. Candace. Her family. Paul. Their marriage. Bob. Their disgusting habits. The girls. The drugs. The money. Romeo.

Her body shuddered as her memory reached Romeo. His eyes as they rested on hers. His hand as it traced her body. Those moments under the duvet when the world seemed just right. The way his shoes hit the pavement and his body followed. The way he loved her. And she, him. Like Marcel.

"Romeo," she said a little too loudly.

"He's okay," Candace replied. Her hands back on her friend. "You both were in an explosion. You both survived. He needed surgery."

Susan's hand felt for the rigid plastic chairs that filled the waiting area. The dimpled surface reassured her that this was real. That Candace was real. That Romeo was going to live.

"It wasn't a dream," she whispered. "It happened."

Candace watched her friend carefully.

"Paul and his slut, Zara." Susan spat as she said the name. "Bob and his whores." She shrugged and straightened her neck. Her chin lifted in defiance. "They are all the same. Paul, Bob, those men all those years ago."

"Shhh," Candace interposed. "Relax. Maybe we should go for a walk? Clear our heads?" The lines on her forehead were deeper than normal.

"No, thanks. I want to be here when Romeo wakes up." Susan shook her hands and feet like a dog that shakes off water. "I'll be fine."

The two returned to their seats and waited. Candace held Susan's hand.

Chapter 40

Paul

Paul was relieved to hear that Susan was still alive. He smirked at himself and his relief when he thought that she had died. How was he able to feel such diametrically opposed emotions and feel that each was real? He sighed and rolled over onto his side. His hand felt Zara's body and instinctively traced the line that once so enchanted him. The sharp drop from her hips to her waist. The sensual line up to her shoulder and down her arm. The gradual line from her waist to her knees. Sunlight pushed back the room's darkness to reveal her raven-black hair and blue eyes, currently closed. He touched the side of her face and received a smile. He kissed her lips.

They made love.

Over coffee, her body warmed from the bath and hotel's robe, Zara put her feet on her lover's lap and crunched on a piece of toast.

"Is there anything that you are afraid of?" She said in near innocent wonder.

Paul loved the near worshiping of him from her. It was one of her most attractive traits. "I'm just a man. I fear like any other." His cryptic answer was supposed to be manly. It sounded flat in the circumstances.

She pouted briefly, then spread her smile across her face. It lit up the room and Paul. "Come-on. Play along. Don't be such a stick in the mud. I want to know what turns you on. And what I can do to protect you." She shifted her feet on his lap and raised her eyebrows.

"You know me as much as I do," Paul replied.

"I don't think that you are afraid of anything," she said. "Except yourself." She added with a smile.

Paul grabbed her foot and squeezed. "You may be on to something." He rubbed for a few seconds as he thought. "My greatest fear…" the words came out as though he was talking to himself. "…is irrelevance." As the words left his mouth, he was surprised at his sincerity. "Being inconsequential and ignored."

Zara leaned forward and put his head between her hands. "You are my sun and moon, silly. How can you ever be irrelevant?"

"I was just joking. Not sure what I was saying." Paul kissed her and put his hands around her. She wrapped her legs around him. He knew that he needed to be needed. To be listened to. To be followed. He didn't want her to know how much she pressed his buttons; how much she turned him on.

"Let's change the subject," she said with a giggle. "Let me take you on a trip. Away from everything."

"I assume I'll be paying for this trip that you take me on?" Paul smiled back.

"Of course. I have something very special planned for us." She kissed his neck, legs still wrapped around his waist. Her hair covered his face briefly. She leaned back and let her robe fall off her shoulders.

"I think that sounds wonderful," Paul said, not hearing his words. His eyes feasted on Zara as he made his way to the bed.

Chapter 41

Bob

Bob fell on the bed, exhausted, next to his favourite from the club. She had been extra attentive during the last few weeks. They sometimes spiced things up with an extra lover. Mainly, they enjoyed a hit of cocaine before and after. Today, Bob lay wide eyed on his back as he recounted recent events. Relating the bombing at the Dorchester to Paul. Combing through the wreckage with Mr Greasy before Paul arrived. Hearing that Greasy turned himself in and admitting everything. What the hell was that about? Accepting, with Paul, that Susan had died. Then, finding out that she was still alive.

"I don't know what I'd do without you," Bob said partly to himself and partly to his lover. Her skin was dark and her hair long. Eyes were blue. German mother, Ethiopian father. Raised in Italy and Rhode Island. Now, a Londoner. Bob wasn't convinced that she told him her real name.

"Or me, you," Lolita said. She stretched her lithe legs alongside his. Their muscles tested each other briefly in response.

"No, really. Things have been tough. Both business and at home."

Lolita raised her eyebrows briefly when he mentioned home. Bob didn't notice.

"That's why you come here, I guess," she kissed him gently before getting up and making her way to the shower. "Hold that thought."

Bob watched her well-defined muscles in her calves and shoulders. She turned to wink at him before disappearing inside the bathroom that contained the shower. She didn't close the door.

After a moment, Bob followed.

Zara

Zara's plan included an ocean-going yacht that they rented and launched from Miami. It included a small crew of four plus themselves. They had their own luxurious cabin and planned on docking in The Bahamas for Paul's business before they began their island hopping through the Caribbean.

"I hope that you aren't expecting me to go full nude," Paul said as he looked at Zara's impeccable skin from the soles of her feet to the top of her head.

She turned her head, eyes flashing in the southern sun. "You can make yourself useful and apply the sunscreen." She lifted her hair to show the nape of her neck and settled into her cushion. A slight sheen highlighted her curves.

They cruised at five knots towards Panama, all business done. Zara glistened with the added lotion and Paul relaxed into his deck chair with cigar and scotch.

He wondered about Bob and how he was supposed to split everything with him. Or Susan. His mood darkened.

Zara, 2

Zara awoke alone in a bed in a room she didn't remember booking. The sun pushed insistently against the heavy block-out curtains. She brushed the hair from her eyes and ran her hands quickly under her covers. No clothes. The flat screen television tilted to allow her a view of the hotel advertising. Someone forgot to turn it off. Waldorf Astoria, it said. The rest of the bed looked unslept in.

She pushed the covers back and found two slippers ready for her. She padded quietly to the bathroom and turned on the shower. An overly fluffy robe was folded, ready for her, next to the shower. There was nothing else. No clothes, no mobile, no money that she could find.

She called the receptionist and received a cheery 'hello', but little else. When she told them that she didn't have any money or clothes, she was quickly put through to the manager.

"Yes, Miss, I understand. But our records clearly show that you and your husband…sorry, partner, booked this apartment weeks ago. Your husband's signature is on the registry."

Zara's head was foggy. "But I don't have any money or clothes. And I don't see him anywhere."

There was a slight hesitation. The manager had seen almost everything in his thirty-two years of service. "I'm sure that there is a simple explanation. I can see that your suite has been paid for the next two weeks. Perhaps your partner has a surprise planned for you?"

Silence from Zara.

"And we can get you some clothes now so that you have something. Our concierge will arrange for everything, including a personal shopper to help you get some more. I'll have her call you for sizes."

"Thank you. That's very kind." Zara sat on the edge of the bed as the words sank in. She hung up and put her hands on her lap and stared at the wall, not seeing. It's happening, she thought.

Chapter 44

Zara, 3

Bob received a call from Zara midafternoon London time.

"How long has he been gone?" he said, the noise of Trafalgar Square's traffic suddenly forgotten.

"Almost a week," Zara replied. "I wouldn't have called but this is not like Paul."

Bob agreed but said nothing. "He hasn't called me. Did you have an argument?"

"No," Zara said frostily.

"Sorry, had to ask. And no chance that he popped out to make some grand gesture?" Bob thought about Susan and marriage. Maybe Paul was stupid enough to ask Zara?

"Look, I wanted to let you know. It's probably nothing. Just that it I haven't seen or heard from him and I thought that he'd be in touch with you if anybody. I just need to know that he's safe. I'm a big girl. I can get on a plane myself if need be."

Bob reassured her and hung up. "Shit," he muttered to himself under his breath. He suddenly felt his collar scratch and he ran his finger along the inside to see what was there. He inhaled as deeply as he could, feeling the limits of his lungs. He scanned the four bronze lions at the base of Nelson's Column, seeing nothing but a red mist and feeling nothing apart from the pulse of his heart in his ears.

Chapter 45

Susan, 2

Susan held Romeo as the phone rang. It had been tough to see him so diminished. The wheelchair out of the hospital. The talks with the physio. The weakened left half of him. Reassurances that he would regain his functions. The realization that sex was still quite good despite the stroke. His smile despite it all. His eyes that still penetrated deep inside her.

"Mrs Derainier?" The voice was formal.

"Yes?" Her voice contained the muffled softness of sleep.

"I'm sorry to have woken you."

Susan became very awake. "I'm awake. How can I help you?"

"It's about your husband, Paul Derainier."

Susan shot a look at Romeo's sleeping form under the duvet. Her chest tingled as though a pitcher of ice water was being poured through an opening in the back of her head. Her chest tightened in response and her palms became slick. She quickly slid out of bed and pressed her mobile tighter to her ear.

"Have you heard from your husband, Mrs Derainier?" The voice continued.

"We are estranged. I haven't been living with him for almost a year." Saying the words made it more real for Susan. It put a faint smile on her lips. The floor suddenly felt harder against her feet. "Has anything happened to him?"

"We can't say at this stage. A missing person's report was lodged and we are following this up."

"Who lodged the report? His girlfriend?" Her body was instantly warm at the thought.

"I'm not sure, ma'am. Just following this up. We'll keep you updated. You'll be on this number?"

"Yes. It is always on me."

"Great." The officer gave her name, number and an email. "If you hear anything, I'd really appreciate a call."

Susan put her phone in her pocket afterwards and walked in a stunned silence to the kitchen. She made green tea for herself and a strong coffee for Romeo with some fruit. She walked back to the bedroom with just her green tea.

Bob, 2

Bob stretched out full length on the bed, Lolita next to him. His arms fell limp next to him. If Paul was gone for real, he thought, then he really would be getting nothing. His head was heavy from the new batch that Lolita gave him. She liked to try different things. It was what kept him interested in her. Her walk or the way her shirt sat askance, showing a collar bone or the muscular curve of her waist as it met her pelvic bones. She excited him with the slow opening of her eyes on him. Or the touch that was soft and insistent. Her body spoke to him with confidence and strength.

An hour or a day later, he rarely kept track, he rolled out of bed and shuffled, naked, to the shower. She knocked on the glass with two cups of coffee, nothing else on. They shared it together in the enormous walk in shower, careful to keep the water out of their cups.

The water and coffee was restorative. His eyes lost the film of drug-induced sleep.

The warehouses that had burned down were to be rebuilt at some point in the near future. They would get their three years' rent from the insurance despite the pandemic-induced vacancy. All was well.

Apart from Paul's disappearance. It was six months and still no news. His girl, Zara, was going out of her mind with worry. Susan even showed some concern but was more interested in her recovering cripple of a boyfriend. How she put up with him he didn't know. He was happy with Lolita. His taste for drugs had expanded to heroin. He was glad that he had someone to share it with. His breathing was shallow and he had lost his tan months ago.

"Are you joining me in the gym today?" Lolita said as she put on her tights with nothing beneath. Her fingertips gently touched her lips to reveal her smiling white teeth.

"I think go without me, sweetheart. I'm not feeling up to it." Bob was still in his robe. He hadn't left the club in days.

"Wouldn't it be better to get some fresh air? Perhaps drive out to your brother's pad in the country?" Her eyes squinted concern.

"Maybe tomorrow. Go and enjoy yourself." He swung his legs back on the bed and reached for the remote. "Do you have any more of that gear from last night?" He had found Netflix and was scrolling through the options.

"Here." She put it on the table next to him. "Be careful, heh?" She wasn't sure whether it was the blue light from the television reflecting off Bob, but she could swear that there was a tinge of blue on his lips. She looked at the blackout curtains but left them closed. With a quick kiss, she left.

"Almost like a girlfriend," Bob thought to himself as he unrolled the needles and heroin. "May need to trade her in. I am starting to get too close."

He found a movie and sat back against three pillows. It wasn't easy to find the vein. As the heroin entered his system, he lost track of his breathing, his brother, even Lolita. All was peaceful.

Chapter 47

Six Months after the explosion

Romeo strained to walk normally. At first, he listed to the left and fell. Even his hand was too weak to support himself. Susan became his support. His reason to live. She removed the shotgun shell from his pocket. She told him that she would give it to him later when he was all better. In the interim, it sat in her safety deposit box in Selfridges.

After three months, he could walk with a cane.

After six, he could walk unaided. He tried to strut but he fell over and thought better of it. Susan hid her smile. They were walking in Regents Park. If he felt well enough, they would go to the zoo.

In front of the gorillas, he fell to the floor. Susan lunged to help. He pushed her back.

"I can do this," he said evenly. He was on all fours, knees and hands against the concrete path. A mother with a pushchair looked back with concern at him.

"You don't need to prove anything, my love." Susan was crouching next to him, trying to not show the concern that she constantly felt when they left their home. She reluctantly stood up and watched him turn towards her.

From all fours, he lifted his left leg up so that he was kneeling. When he turned his face to hers, he was holding a small red box. The mother that was watching with concern stopped suddenly and swivelled to watch. A Chinese tour group slowed their approach as their guide recognised and quickly translated what was happening. Within seconds, there was a small crowd that gathered at a not-so respectful distance.

"What are you doing, Romeo?" The words caught in Susan's throat as tears welled up. Her body shook from explosions of adrenaline. Her breathing increased and she became rooted to the ground.

Romeo took her hand and looked at her in the face. "Susan, from the moment you entered my life, I knew it would never be the same. A lot has happened since you asked me. But I felt that I should also ask you as we haven't really spoken about it since that day." His voice quivered slightly as a shadow passed over his face. "You are my everything. Susan, will you marry me?"

A single tear ran down the cheek of the mother and child, also frozen in their spot. The Chinese tour held their breath as one, half videoing the event with their phones. Susan could no longer see Romeo through her tears. Her head nodded and she said, "Yes. A million times yes."

Romeo slid a four carat diamond ring onto Susan's trembling finger. Little rainbows burst from her finger as she looked at it. She closed her hand over his and pulled him towards her. They kissed and held each other for a long time. It took a while for them to feel the slaps of congratulations from the strangers who watched. The mother smiled at them and to herself as she turned and continued her way. The Chinese tour surrounded them and congratulated themselves with photos and commentaries. The couple shook hands and smiled for each photo in turn.

Only the gorilla seemed unimpressed.

Chapter 48

Bob, 3

Paul remained missing. Susan's divorce was approved, and Lolita wanted to move in with Bob.

"Why not go to your brother's country estate? At least until he comes back? You look like you can do with the rest." She took his hands and put it against her cheek. His bluish fingertips gently caressed her waxy complexion.

"It feels like giving up, you know? The Club is fine."

"It's not fine," she said between kisses. "You need more than just excitement. We both need more than the Club. You need to get well." She pulled him closer. She could feel his bones through his clothes.

"I need to be available for the police if they learn anything," Bob said.

"They can phone you or visit you on the estate. Same with the investigators."

Bob pulled away and slumped his shoulders. "It's as though he disappeared. And he didn't say a thing to me. I don't like it. It doesn't smell right."

Lolita's eyes opened wide, then closed slowly. "I'm sure it's fine. He needed to get away."

"You don't know him. He doesn't do this. He's the safe pair of hands." His mind drifted to the Salisbury House café all those years ago with his hands on his brothers.

"Bob." She stopped and forced him to look at her. "You need help. Your life is a wreck. We need to get out of this place. If you don't, you'll die. And you'll never see Paul."

Bob started at her bluntness. She was his. Not for him to listen to or obey her.

"Look, Lolita. Let's not forget where we are and who you are."

"Bastard," she hissed.

"We are in a brothel. I have paid good money for you to care for me. And you have done a marvellous job. I really care for you as well. But we are not a couple, understand?"

Lolita was silent. Her eyes looked at a space on the floor.

"In fact, I need a hit. Set me up and leave me alone." He turned his back to her and made his way to the sofa in front of the television.

She put a package next to him and walked out. He watched her until he heard the door click shut.

When she returned two hours later, she found him asleep on the sofa. His face was bluer than normal. She crawled under the covers and waited for him. When she awoke, he was still on the sofa. He hadn't moved.

He was dead.

Chapter 49

Susan got the call the next day. She went and identified the body. She called Bob's parents. They already knew about Paul's absence. They arranged for Bob's body to be returned home to Canada where he was buried with full rights in the Churchyard of the family town. Paul had donated heavily to the church and the entire family had spaces reserved for them. No newspaper or blog mourned Bob's death. He passed without notice into the great void. Susan remained in London. She was getting married.

The stones of the drive crunched under the weight of their carriage. Open. Blue Sky. Very little breeze. Her dress was modern, white, and lacked the flourishes that her first wedding captured so well in pictures. The registry was small with yellow light that made the oak-panelled walls even darker. The pleasant woman who officiated smiled and said her words. They said their words. They kissed. They signed. They left. Only Candace and her family witnessed the ceremony. Their reception was held in the family's favourite restaurant: Le Gavroche in Mayfair, London.

Their honeymoon was South Africa. Umhlanga.

The waves crashed into the stones below as they closed the doors overlooking the vast expanse of ocean that met with the horizon. Susan turned and walked towards her husband, her negligée caressing her body. Romeo kissed her and pulled her towards him. They danced in silence as the sun touched the sea, giving the newlyweds an orange and yellow sky as a wedding present. Romeo had forgotten his shotgun shell long ago. Susan had not forgotten Marcel, but the memories of that day became merged with this. The bad had been finally erased.

Two years after the Explosion

Paul scrambled to find a piece of clothing to cover his nakedness. A layer of dust covered his body, hiding the excrement and urine that he was subjected to earlier. They had gone for now, but would probably return, he thought. The shower's warmth washed the event and memory away. While terrible, it was no longer shocking. That day was nearly two years ago when he woke up on a bed, in a locked room, with no carpet, windows, or even running water.

His head was foggy and sore, his body dehydrated. His room-mate was screaming and banging on the door. A guard came and opened it. Both were pulled out. They were separated. He was escorted to a room with a steel door and a large mirror. He assumed that it was a two-way mirror with others observing him from the other side. There was a steel chair and steel table, secured to the floor with a welded piece of metal and heavy bolts. He lost track of time before the door opened and two large men in white jackets walked in followed by a man six inches shorter than himself in a cotton suit. He assumed that this was the warden or boss of some sort. He first noticed his moustache. Then, the tanned skin with inquisitive eyes. Like a rat, he thought. And the receding hair that showcased a tanned head. The hair was cut short, like a marine's. In his hands was a clipboard and a pen.

"Name?" His voice was higher than expected and Paul had to do a double take.

"Paul."

"Do you know why you are here?" The person was not prepared to introduce himself or give any further explanation to Paul.

"I'm not sure where here is, sir," Paul said in his most deferential tone.

The man in the cotton suit looked up from his clipboard for the first time. "Are you trying to test me, Paul?"

The two looked at each other, unblinking. Paul looked away first.

"No, sir."

"Then tell me why you are here." The eyes bore through him. Blackened rods of steel that betrayed nothing.

"I honestly don't know," said Paul truthfully. His body was no longer sore from whatever drug he took or was given. It pulsed with anger and fear. His mind raced to determine who could be behind this.

"Interesting," the man said. He wrote something down and turned the page. "Do you know how long you have been here?"

"I just awoke and here I was," Paul explained. "I don't know how I got here. The last thing I remember…"

"Enough of that. I think that I've heard enough for now. I'll be watching you, Paul." To the guards, he nodded and walked out the door.

Paul was left alone but not for long. Another guard, also in a white jacket, escorted him to a new room that contained a toilet and two bunks.

"Is this a jail?" Paul asked.

The guard closed the door half way before smirking. He was about to say something, then changed his mind. Paul heard the guard's footsteps as he turned to see who was in the bunk.

A large man covered in tattoos with no discernible hair lay motionless on the top of a grey blanket. His head turned to watch his intruder take a step towards him.

"Hi, I'm Paul." Looking at his situation, he felt it best to be the peacekeeper.

"Did I ask your name?" He swung his legs over and unfolded himself to stand next to Paul. He was nearly six inches taller. He was not wearing any clothes. Paul scanned and realised that his tattoos were over every square inch of his body.

"I'm new here. I'm not looking for any trouble. I just need to talk to my lawyer and we'll get this all sorted out."

The tattoo man laughed. It sounded feral. Paul felt the front of his trousers warm. He looked down to see the growing stain. The man laughed harder.

"I'm not your lawyer. I'm your worst nightmare."

The words were barely spoken when Paul felt a fist against his face. It was the first time he had ever been hit like that. No warning. No reason. The second went into the gut and Paul hit the floor. The third was a kick that knocked him unconscious. When he awoke, his clothes were torn and some cast against the wall. He was alone. Dried blood ran the entire length of his leg. His trousers were gone and he felt the beginnings of bruises on his thighs and arms. He reached behind him and gingerly touched the source of the blood.

His body began to shake from rage and fear. He screamed at the top of his lungs for some help. Nothing in reply. Not even another prisoner to mock his cries. The pain was dull at first, then unbearable as the body tried to heal itself. As the body tried to warn him of its injuries. As the body screamed for help.

When both he and his body realised that there was no help, he curled up against the wall and began to cry.

Chapter 51

Prison

A bottle of water was thrown inside his door later that day along with a tray of colourless food. The next day, he was taken back to the same room and met with the same two guards in white jackets and the man with the moustache.

"Do you know why you are here?" asked the man.

"Do you know who I am?" asked Paul. "I am an important man outside of these walls. I can pay you whatever you want. Whatever you are being paid, I can treble it."

The man looked at Paul with his black eyes. "Delusional. Shame."

"I am rich," Paul said, moving his eyes between each of the three men in front of him. "I can pay." When that didn't work, he asked to see his lawyer. Again, a smirk from the moustache man.

"Take Paul to his new home," the man said to the men in white jackets. His head was bent downwards as he read something else on the paper before he turned and disappeared behind the steel door.

Paul was taken to his new room. The hallways smelled of antiseptic with a hint of faeces. His room had no smell that he could detect on entering. There was a single bed, a sink, and a metal toilet. No outside window. The only glass was the size of a postcard at eye level in a steel door, covered with a sliding piece of metal. Guards could check on him but he could see nothing.

The two large guards in white coats sat him down at the edge of his bed. Before he could react, they stuck a needle into his arm. It was through the fabric of his clothing. No disinfectant before or plaster afterwards. They grunted for him to lie down. He obeyed. They nodded their heads and the room went black.

When he awoke, there was a tray of food on the floor just inside the door. He ate. Same colourless and tasteless food as the day before. There was a paper cup with two pills inside. One was white, the other red.

The door opened and the guard noticed that the pills had not been taken.

"Take your pills."

Paul shrugged.

"You need to take this or else I have to make you take them," the guard said in what came close to a sympathetic tone.

"How are you going to do that?" Paul asked before he thought it through.

The guard's head disappeared and two other guards appeared. One held a syringe. The other held leather restraints.

Paul took his pills and put his head on the bed to rest.

The door clicked shut and he was alone. Outside his door he heard whimpering and crying. The screams came without warning and ceased just as quickly.

Two years passed without him keeping track. It could have been ten. He had no visitors. No solicitor. No contact with the outside world.

When he was grabbed by a naked man covered in his own urine and faeces, he punched and scratched until he broke free. In the process, he ran into the yard under the intense summer sun. The grass was brown and the trees were surrounded by dirt turned into dust through neglect. He fell and rolled into a ball as two other residents started screaming and kicking him when he invaded their space. They tore off his remaining clothes. The naked man covered in faeces caught up and grabbed him again. He bit Paul on his bicep and calf.

The guards let the residents fight.

When Paul finally freed himself and the screaming stopped, the naked man was rocking on the ground in a foetal position. He was now also naked and needed a shower. Without complaint or comment, he walked to the showers to clean himself off.

Chapter 52

The Circle Closes

Susan's soft scented hair covered her shoulders like a cape. Her tanned skin highlighted the whites of her eyes and teeth. Her hand rested delicately in Romeo's as they strolled through the Heath before having tea in Kenwood House. Their Honeymoon was perfect and Marcel had been laid to rest in Susan's heart and mind.

"You go ahead, sweetheart," Susan said to Romeo as they neared the café. "Get me whatever you are having. I'll be five minutes."

Romeo leaned in and kissed her gently, barely touching her lips. His hands brushed her hips and came up to her shoulders like a summer breeze through a bed of flowers. He smiled and ducked inside. His limp almost gone. His cane replaced with an umbrella.

Susan looked at her husband for a moment after he had disappeared. Her face held a smile as enigmatic as the Mona Lisa's. Her eyes drifted towards the trees in the distance and saw the figure she was waiting for. She raised her eyebrows in recognition and lifted her hand slightly. The other did the same.

They closed the distance between themselves and stopped two paces apart. Susan's hair reflected a golden light. The other woman's raven-black hair flashed in the early afternoon sunlight. The stranger was young, early thirties, athletic, and glowing with health. She hesitated slightly before extending her hand.

"Nice to finally meet you, Susan." She forced a smile as her cold hand was enveloped by the warmth of Susan's.

"Nice to finally meet you, Zara."

Susan held her hand a moment too long. She could feel the strength in the grip. The youth and energy that she would never feel again. The woman Paul fell in love with. The woman Susan wanted Paul to fall in love with.

They both turned away from Kenwood House and talked with heads slightly downcast. Shoulder to shoulder, they looked like they were examining the ground for a lost piece of jewellery.

"Any news?" Zara couldn't hold back her burning question.

"About Paul?"

She looked at Susan as though she were looking over a pair of reading glasses.

"Yes, of course," Susan stammered. She didn't think that it would be so difficult to talk to Zara. Paul was a letch, a thief, and a low-life. She was a money-grabbing whore who was prepared to destroy a marriage for her fancy. And yet she was young and beautiful and took Paul all by herself. No help was needed. "It's been well over two years and not a pip. I have instructed a firm of forensic accountants to search through his financial holdings and dealings. It is my position that all of this is mine."

"Or, at least, half," Zara said.

"Our deal stands. It is not up for negotiation," snapped Susan.

"OK. I wasn't suggesting anything."

"Don't be clever. You've done a job. You'll be paid as agreed."

"I know."

Susan paused, not sure if that was a threat or an acknowledgment.

"There is one more thing to do. Are you sure you are able to carry it out?" Susan was astonished that she was having second thoughts. Maybe she should let him rot in that place, she thought.

"Of course. Upon payment in full."

"I need to get things resolved with the accountants and the courts first."

"Understood." Zara's hair tangled in the wind and she pulled it deftly and twisted it into a bun with a clip that emerged from nowhere. "But I'd like to finish this. I didn't think that it'd take so long."

Susan looked over her shoulder and scanned the horizon for eavesdroppers. "Ten years was always going to be a long time. I can't make an application declaring him dead until then."

"And you want him to stay in that place instead of providing some level of mercy? A simple needle will take away all of his pain and torture that he is experiencing." Zara's eyes watered, betraying her tough talk.

"I'll leave it to you. I am divorced and disinterested in Paul. But I am also the sole beneficial owner of his estate. I am happy to wait." Susan touched the faded scar around her neck. A memory of Bob in her bedroom flashed across her face. Of Paul in the Club with Bob. Of Paul with his whore Zara in Susan's marital bed or the hotel near the golf club.

Zara touched her lips and rubbed her nose.

"I'll sort it out." She nodded to Susan and walked in the opposite direction.

Susan watched her disappear into the treed walks. Taking a couple of breaths, she turned and walked back to Romeo. She hoped that the clotted cream was fresh today.

Chapter 53

Butterfly wings

Susan held the baby puppy on his back, tickling its feet and tummy. It was the same breed as Sable. A little black highlighted its face, accenting its lion-like golden eyes. Its brindle coloured fur was spotted with white on its chest and paws. She put baby Sable next to her neck and felt the little kisses tickle her flesh.

Romeo was in the City on business and she was lazing the morning away. Her mind drifted to the moment she stumbled across those papers in Paul's home office. She wasn't looking for anything more than a USB stick for her computer. She opened every drawer and door, hoping to see something that resembled a USB so that she could download her movies to take with her and Candace to Paris the following week.

She put the USB in her laptop and found unencrypted folders. She opened them to see names and companies that she had never heard about. Accountants and fiduciaries complete with locations, banks, account numbers.

Her body froze with the uncertainty of what she was seeing. She quickly copied the contents of the USB and put it back exactly where she found it.

Over the years, she was able to piece together a better picture of what was going on. Holidays in the Channel Islands or Hong Kong or Singapore or even Panama with a quick meeting at the local bank or solicitor's office. A job that she never fully understood. Bob's role in everything. The money with no credible history. She handed the details she discovered to the forensic accountants when Paul went missing and someone was needed to step into his shoes.

The role for Zara was inspired and purely accidental. The current plan evolved after Bob and Paul showed their true colours. It was supposed to scare them. Until she realised that they wouldn't scare. Or change. Then they tried to kill her. Or, at least were happy when they thought that she was dead. There was only one solution.

She was pleased when Mr Greasy fell on his sword. Very rarely does a stalker come to be so handy as him. She was Mr X. She intended to be in the blast but not to nearly die. That was never the plan. Her man with the bombs was a little too good at what he knew. It was terrifying what money and contacts can achieve.

She ran her fingers along the scar that changed her life so completely. That made her capable of what she had done. Or could do. For her, it was done for love.

Chapter 54

Freedom

Paul dragged his numb leg as he made his way to the canteen. It was a treat to eat with other people. He held firm to the wall's railing as he made his way to the table. A man in a white jacket got him a tray of colourless and tasteless food and placed it in front of Paul. He ate it heartedly.

The fog would clear on certain days and he could swear that he had been set up. He explained that he was on first name basis with the former prime minister of Britain. That he had over a £100 million pounds in banks throughout the world. And that he had done nothing to deserve being placed in such an austere and cruel mental facility. He determined that he was somewhere in Central America. Guatemala? Who knew. No one was telling.

He finished his food and nodded to the guard who helped him to the wall. Paul dragged himself back to his room. The door was left open. He always took his medications. He lay down on his bed and stared at the ceiling. Very little passed through his mind lately.

An unfamiliar shuffle caused him to look up and towards his door. A different guard in a white jacket filled the space. He smiled, so Paul smiled back.

"Everything okay with you today, Paul?" The guard's voice was higher than his bulk would suggest. He was otherwise pleasant and sympathetic to Paul.

"Yes, sir."

"Have you had any visitors recently?"

Paul shifted and sat up abruptly. "Visitors?" His breathing increased and he felt his heartbeat against his chest.

"Of course. Our training said that everyone was entitled to visitors and a call per week. Do you have anyone you'd like to call?"

Paul's mouth went dry and his eyes welled up with tears. "Uh, yes, please." He couldn't remember how long he had been in captivity but he did remember that he had some people outside.

"How about your wife? Or girlfriend? Or would you prefer your lawyer?"

Paul sensed a shift in the air. The guard was smiling and standing next to him. Too close. He wanted to stand but feared any repercussions.

"All three if possible." Paul was shaking. Only his bad leg was still.

The man in the white jacket pulled out a mobile phone and handed it to Paul. "Would this do?"

Paul couldn't focus as he held the phone in his hands. It was unlocked and he began dialling Susan's number. When it began to ring, he could barely hold the phone from nerves.

"Hello?" It was Susan's voice.

"Hello?" Susan repeated herself.

The needle delivered its intended load into the jugular of Paul. The effect was immediate. Paul never felt the needle nor heard Susan's voice.

fins

ABOUT THE AUTHOR

Baron was born in Canada.
He currently lives in South-East England,
somewhere near the Surry/Sussex borders.
Sightings vary.

If you'd like to follow Baron and receive free samples
of his future writing before it is published, please visit
www.baronalexanderbooks.com

www.ingramcontent.com/pod-product-compliance
Lightning Source LLC
Chambersburg PA
CBHW030806200726
48285CB00015B/1506